TRAIL OF THE TALON

JACK GANNON
CYNDI WILLIAMS-BARNIER

ISBN-13: 979-8-9852082-1-4

YBR PUBLISHING, LLC

Jack Gannon   Co-Owner, Production Manager
Cyndi Williams-Barnier - Co-Owner, Marketing Manager
Bill Barnier – Co-Owner, Senior Editor
Loreen Ridge-Husum – Art Director

REVIEW

5-Star Award

Task Force Agent Calvin "Seeker" Geffers and FBI Special Agent Stephanie Anderson were vacationing at a beach hotel in Charleston when they received the call. Seeker and Stephanie must find and rescue a girl kidnapped from her home. On the hunt, they faced off with Talon, the most wanted elusive international criminal and extortionist. No one saw him and lived, but there'd always be an exception to this rule. Talon was always a step ahead, and the duo raced against time to stop him. From America to Argentina and the places in between, they tailed Talon to stop the next crime. And while at it, romance, discoveries, and drama took center stage in Trail of the Talon by Jack Gannon and Cyndi Williams-Barnier. Who would go down first? The couple or Talon?

"Trail of The Talon" by Jack Gannon and Cyndi Williams-Barnier was a tale of romance, survival, action, humor, and drama. The novel was a mix of James Bond's signature and wonder-kid vibe. I loved the plot, development, and storyline. I also laughed a lot, especially when Seeker and Stephanie banter. And even while I laughed, the sensitive situation struck me. Niklas was a product of his circumstance, and I felt pain for the child. But did his past justify the present? The thought gave me a pause. Ms. Murphy was a minor character, but she left a lasting impression. I love tough women. Finally, our protagonists were the stars of this show. Seeker and his resourceful yet unpredictable gadgets got a yes from me. I also enjoyed seeing Stephanie in action and with her wit intact, even in the face of danger. Together, they were a formidable team. Thank you, Jack and Cyndi, for a beautiful book.

~Jennifer Ibiam, Readers' Favorite, LLC

PROLOGUE

Previously in "The Task Force That Saved Christmas":

Task Force Agent Calvin "Seeker" Geffers and FBI Special Agent Stephanie Anderson relaxed in their hotel room on Folly Beach, just south of Charleston, South Carolina. They were still in bed after a wonderfully romantic night, and she got up just long enough to make them each a cup of coffee before getting back under the sheets with him. "Wow," she said. "Don't think we've gone a whole three months without an argument before." She rolled off his chest to kiss his cheek. "I love you."

He kissed her in return. "I love you back."

His cell phone rang first, with hers joining in seconds later. Instinct told both to answer their summons. "Seeker," he said. "Agent Anderson," she said. They answered their calls and hung up.

"Raincheck on another day in bed?" Calvin said as he got up and went to his suitcase, removing his black Task Force uniform.

"Hope to be back here in a couple hours myself," she said as she started putting on her bulletproof vest and blouse, forgetting her bra in the urgency. As she tugged up her panties and reached for her black slacks, Kevlar vest, blouse and jacket, she asked, "How long does it normally take you to solve a kidnapping, anyway?"

He zipped up his uniform front and waved his gloved hand over the closure for the controls in his palm to bio-magnetically seal it. "Always too long…"

CHAPTER 1

Bullets ricocheted off the crates above them in the late afternoon summer sunshine, sending fine wood powder and splinters down on their heads.

"Damn it, I keep forgetting to requisition that hood." Seeker instinctively held his arm up to shield his face from the falling debris. "This crap is gettin' in my 'do."

Anderson stared over at Seeker in disbelief. "What? We're getting shot at and all you're worried about is that nappy head of yours?"

Seeker ducked down as more bullets splintered the crates and sent wood flying. He was wearing the multi-purpose cocoon glasses the agency created for all the field agents, and his vision was completely unobstructed by the falling particles. As he fired his weapon back at their attackers he said, "'Nappy'? Woman, this 'do cost me a hundred fifty dollars. Wanted to look my best for our vacation! It's naturally curly, not nappy. My momma's white, and my daddy's—" and ducked down as more bullets dinged over his head "—beautifully caramel, just like me."

Anderson formed a slight grin as she ducked down also. She just learned something new about him. She enjoyed any time she could pick on him, even in a heated shootout. She was well aware that he was particular about his clothing (when not in his black uniform) and his preened hair. His light brown skin, green eyes and beautiful locks were what attracted her to him to begin with. She never knew he once wore very short hair when he was in the military. There wasn't much she *did* know about the mysterious man in their fiery love/hate relationship. "My momma's white, too, y'know. How'd you think I got this blonde hair and blue eyes, pretty boy?"

He peered around the side of the large crate that protected them from the incoming gunfire, but as soon as he did, more bullets began splintering the wood.

"Will you keep your head back here?" she growled at him. "Damn, you're worse than a husband!"

"How would you know? You don't have a husband."

"Well, it's not like I haven't given you plenty of chances."

Seeker scowled at her.

The bullet barrage abruptly stopped. Seeker withdrew a special device from one of the black canvas pouches on his gun belt and activated the unit. Its screen immediately glowed with colored dots. "Not good," he said. He watched as four green dots moved closer to two white dots on the biometric radar screen. "They're coming toward us." He quickly surveyed the dock area around them, then looked at Anderson, and stuffed the meter back in place. "Okay, blue eyes, feel like goin' for a swim?" The only escape route was straight back, off the dock and into the harbor water, twenty feet down.

"Oh, no you don't." She shook her head. "You've gotta be kidding! This is a brand-new suit!"

"And since when do special agents afford Armani pant-suits anyway?"

"When we don't have husbands to coddle, we have extra disposable cash…what did you think?"

He holstered his weapon, hurriedly opened a different belt pouch, and removed two collapsible rebreathers specially manufactured by Jason Enterprises for the Task Force. He handed one to Anderson. "This'll give you about three minutes of air."

She said in return, "Do you know what saltwater does to a gun, Seeker?"

"Rebreather, *now!*"

Anderson saw the determination in Seeker's eyes; she knew he was not fooling around, and now was not the time for their usual banter. She holstered her Beretta, locked it in place and stuffed the rebreather in her mouth, just in time to have Seeker push her over the end of the dock and down into the murky salt waters below.

Seeker removed another pouch and withdrew both of its contents. He activated the device, secured it with putty, and slammed it against the face of their protective crate and followed Anderson into the water.

Under the water, Seeker grabbed Anderson's arms to keep her from surfacing. His cocoons immediately sealed against his skin when he encountered the water. The glasses were a highly developed device, worn by each agent, day, or night, when on a mission. The device performed innumerable tasks including night vision capabilities, environmental readings, and examining substances, but now they served as modified goggles aiding Seeker to see clearly through the murky waters.

Anderson was essentially blinded by the cloudiness and the salt water stung her eyes. Knowing she was fairly helpless in the situation, she allowed Seeker to guide her along. Less than a minute after their descent, they heard a muffled explosion and the water began to ripple above them. The murkiness brightened and large pieces of crate and dock planking splashed into the water.

Anderson felt the concussion and her body jerked in response. She thought, "*Seeker. He did something again...I know he did! Probably something I'm sure I'll regret when we surface.*"

Seeker continued to maneuver their submerged position to avoid the sharp missiles of wood jetting downward.

Their short air supplies began to run low and both started to feel lightheaded. Anderson felt a sudden pang of panic, and also felt him guide her up to the surface toward one of the several loading dock pilings. Their heads broke through the surface of the water, and both spit out the rebreathers and let them sink below the surface. Anderson gulped in fresh air, breathing harder than she should have, and her dizziness increased momentarily. She thought about scolding Seeker for the entire daunting situation. She opened her mouth to speak, and Seeker placed a gloved index finger on her lips.

"Shhh," Seeker whispered. "Could be more of 'em up there. Just follow me."

They remained silent and slowly treaded water, advancing quietly toward the shore underneath the dock and pilings. Within moments they felt the muddy ground under their feet and stepped out of the water. Instinctively, they both drew their guns. Anderson grimaced as she watched water drip from her weapon. She thought momentarily about the hours it would take to disassemble it, clean it with fresh water, dry it out, oil it, and put it back together. She considered the payback Seeker would have to suffer later.

Anderson looked back toward the dock from which they had jumped. A mangled mess of pilings and some lumber was all that was left of their former protective shielding.

"What the hell did you do?" she whispered to him.

"Left a surprise behind," he whispered back. "At the very least our odds should be much better now. It'll be easier to find the girl with less goons hangin' around."

Anderson's anger left as swiftly as it had begun. She grabbed him around his neck with her free hand, and a surprised Seeker was rewarded with a passionate kiss. He felt her tongue probe his teeth for just a moment before she pulled back. The adrenaline from their escape combined with the sudden kiss from Anderson made his pulse quicken. His attention temporarily left the battle scene and stirred an arousal of thoughts about the blonde woman standing before him. Just as sudden, he shook his head rapidly to clear the fog from his brain. Droplets of water flew from his wet hair. "Not now," he complained softly. "As hot as you look standing there, all wet and damned sexy-looking, we've got bad guys to catch and a girl to rescue."

She whispered back, "Well, I needed to 'thank you' for saving my ass again. It seems this is becoming a habit. And I'm so gonna deck you for ruining my suit."

The two made their way to the edge of the dock's underside. Anderson found herself enjoying the backside view of Seeker's muscular body in its wet black uniform. It was form-fitting to start with, as a standard protective operations reason, but now wet it heightened every muscular angle. *Just wait till I get you alone later,* she thought.

She heard the sound of her feet squishing with every step in her black flats. She stopped a moment to take off her shoes and leave them on the ground so she couldn't be heard.

She wished right then that she hadn't polished her toenails in bright red the night before. It wasn't professional. She was supposed to be on vacation, however, with intentions to enjoy herself with the mysterious, also-off-duty Seeker.

Despite the years she'd known him, and the few official times their paths crossed, she'd contemplated the fact that she knew very little about the man, except his special agent name, that he was part of a secret federal Task Force, and he infuriated her every time they worked a case together. He'd been the only man she could say she actually lusted after, ever. He was someone who kissed her with soft passionate kisses, ones that made her body melt, and she was uncharacteristically submissive to him…she had never given in to any man who had intentions with her until she met Seeker, until she began this intoxicating affair with him. When they made love, he could make her tingle from her toes all the way up. Then he'd be off onto another one of his classified missions. He was a man she could and couldn't have at the same time and it infuriated her. She couldn't make up her mind whether she despised him or loved him, or both.

They climbed up the wood supports and crossbeams of the dock bracing, with Seeker leading the way. As he neared the access opening to the dock's surface, he looked back toward the waterside edge. He, too, saw the crate where they had been hiding was now blown to smithereens, as were several crates that had been near it, and that area of the dock was gone and there was a crooked semi-circular area of destruction where his surprise bomb went off. There were a few bodies lying unmoving on the dock surface near the blast area, and two men stood over them facing the water; he wondered how they avoided his fatal surprise. Seeker looked toward the warehouse building and saw two more men standing guard in front of a limousine.

Realizing they could possibly be seen, and probably heard, from their position, he lowered his head and turned to Anderson. He made a "two" sign with his left hand, then pointed left and right, to tell her the enemy counts in both directions. She nodded back, and without speaking, she climbed up to Seeker's side. When they were head-to-head she nodded "ready", and they both climbed up as fast as they could, leaping through the access opening onto the dock surface.

Standing back-to-back, they aimed and fired at both pairs of men, sending all four to the ground, dead. Seeker took off at full speed toward the limousine as it started moving, firing at the tires. The driver attempted to speed away, but stopped the car when the tires made deep, popping, explosive sounds as the Glock bullets broke the rubber surfaces and the pressurized air escaped. With the vehicle not drivable, the driver got out and began to run, disappearing behind a small warehouse. Seeker watched as Anderson easily passed him in a full-on barefoot run. She tossed her water-heavy jacket off to the side and increased her sprint speed after the man.

Seeker got to the rear doors of the limousine and opened one by the handle. Seeing the rear compartment was empty, he rested his arm on the top of the door for support, aiming his gun toward the other side of the warehouse, assuming the driver would dart out any second, and assuming Anderson hadn't taken him down first. As seconds passed and no one rounded the opposite corner, he gritted his teeth and said, "Shit!" and ran in pursuit of Anderson and the driver.

Moments earlier, Anderson panted hard as she rounded the corner of the warehouse and sweat combined with sea water glistened on her forehead. The driver was an excellent runner, staying just a few feet in front of her.

The driver looked back as he ran, and saw Anderson come to an abrupt stop and take aim.

She wasn't taking aim at him, though. She wanted him alive, thinking the limo driver may have information on the missing girl. She needed to stop him and saw the perfect opportunity. A group of LP tanks sat next to the warehouse. She measured her quarry's distance from the tanks. She fired once but missed the tanks.

"*No!*" he yelled when he saw what she was aiming at.

Her second shot hit a tank perfectly. The concussion from the explosion sent her man flying off, landing on his back with a hard thud near a large trash dumpster.

By the time his vision cleared Anderson was standing over him, her bare foot pressed against his windpipe. "Nice toes, bitch," he gasped.

"Make one move, asshole, and my gorgeous toes will be the last thing you ever see." She emphasized her threat by pointing her Beretta at his face. He closed his eyes in surrender.

The smile on her face ended abruptly when she felt something metallic poke into the back of her neck. "Drop it, if you please," said a soft male voice in a slight German accent.

Anderson cursed herself as she closed her eyes, moved her finger off her gun's trigger, and tossed it away to her right. She realized this new character had to have been hiding behind a crate or other object behind the warehouse and took advantage of the moment to sneak up on her from behind. The man on the ground gently took her foot in one hand, kissed her big toe, and then angrily pushed her foot off his throat.

"Young man, please go retrieve that truck," said the voice again, to the driver. "And make sure you don't screw this one up, hmmm?" The driver pushed his aching body off the ground and headed toward a warehouse truck a couple dozen yards away. "Turn around, my dear," he said to her.

Anderson complied, and her eyes widened when she saw his face in person for the first time. Before now, she had only seen The Talon's face in Interpol files' few pictures of the international extortionist. His real name was unknown, not unlike agent Seeker. His calling card for every kidnapping or major robbery or espionage was a gold eagle's claw cloisonne pin left at the scene of the crime. For a moment, she felt excited at the thought of arresting this international kidnapper single-handedly, until she remembered he had a gun pointed at her face, and she had tossed her gun a good six feet away.

The Talon was tall, slender and had dark-blond hair. He looked about forty-five years old and was impeccably dressed in a dark blue three-piece suit with a white shirt, matching tie, and expensive Brunello Cuccinelli patent-leather oxford shoes. On his lapel was a gold eagle's claw cloisonné pin. In one hand, he held a Swiss Sphinx 3000 pointed at her forehead. His other hand gripped the hair of a teenage girl. Lizzy Neland, eighteen-years-old with pixie-cut black hair, was the one Anderson and Seeker had been charged to find. Lizzy's hands were tied behind her, her mouth was gagged, and she wore a short pink nightgown with matching panties. She'd been kidnapped from her bedroom three nights earlier. Her father, Garrison Neland, was a wealthy Wall Street investor, and guided many of his clients to great returns on their investments. His own portfolio had grown exponentially in return. When Lizzy was kidnapped from her bedroom in the middle of the night, there was a note left with the signature pin, instructing him to not contact the police and wait for a subsequent message.

When The Talon spoke, his voice sounded as though it were speaking a child's nursery rhyme. "I am impressed, madam," he said. "You are actually the first police official to get this close to me." He gave a respectful nod to Anderson, never breaking his eye-to-eye lock on her. "And as such, I am also honored by such dedication to find me, and this lovely child." He took a few steps backward, forcing Lizzy back with him, jerking at her hair. She stumbled in her bare feet on the rough concrete surface. She gave a muffled squeal through the gag. His eyes scanned the perimeter. "Where is your friend? The one in the black uniform?"

"Knowing him," Anderson said calmly, "he's probably right behind you."

The Talon smiled. "You do realize, madam, that is, as you say, 'the oldest trick in the book'."

"It's only a trick if it works," Anderson replied.

He rotated Lizzy by her hair to face behind him, his Sphinx still pointed at Anderson's forehead. "Is there anyone behind me, child? Speak true, please," he asked softly, eyes still locked on Anderson. Lizzy sniffed and slightly shook her head "no". "Ah, so my choice now is to believe my prey or not. You know, madam, this whole affair is making me late for my evening cocktail." He waved his Sphinx down. "On your knees, please, if you don't mind."

Anderson moved slowly, setting her right foot back, keeping the tips of her toes touching the concrete. She gained a runner's crouch, and grinned…

…as there was a tap on The Talon's right shoulder. Instinctively he looked to his right, into the face of Seeker, his weapon abruptly pressed against The Talon's nose. Immediately Anderson ran forward, grabbing Lizzy by the waist. The surprise of Seeker's presence and Anderson's movement caused The Talon to release his grip on Lizzy's hair just enough for Anderson's inertia to free the teenager with no injury.

"Please, give me a reason to shoot," said Seeker through gritted teeth. "My boss keeps threatening to send me to target practice, and I really have better things to do with my time."

"Oh, my," said The Talon, as calm as before. "I do believe we have a small problem." He purposefully rotated his own gun hand outward, giving Seeker full view of his hand. In his palm, held in place by the Sphinx' handgrip, was a detonator with a dead man's switch. Seeker recognized the model and knew its range was very far…too far for the women to escape in time, and he suspected a booby trap.

"Stephanie!" he yelled at the running agent and Lizzy. "Stop!" Anderson and Lizzy both came to a halt.

The Talon smiled and turned his gun to Seeker. "I see you have an appreciation for such devices as well, smart man that you are."

The driver had hot-wired the warehouse truck and pulled up near the four people. "Please, sir, throw your weapon into that large trash bin, and your holster, too." Seeker knew he could only comply, tossing his weapon into the large dumpster. His gloved hands went to the flat metal buckle with the circle-in-a-circle emblem in its center, pressed in the top and bottom edges to release the lock. With one hand, he tossed his gun belt into the dumpster. "Not that I don't trust you, sir, but the glasses, too. I like to read people's eyes, you see." Once more, Seeker silently obeyed and tossed his cocoons into the trash. "Now, sir, please turn around. Hands behind your back." Seeker followed instruction, and the driver tied his hands with a piece of rope from the truck bed. "Now, please call the females back over."

"Stephanie," said Seeker, "come back over, both of you, nice and slow."

Anderson and Lizzy came back and stood beside Seeker. The driver had picked up Anderson's Beretta and kept it pointed at them as The Talon used his free hand to lock the dead man's switch and place the electronic detonator in his pocket. He stepped forward and pulled up the hem of Lizzy's teddy. Attached to her bare stomach was the remote explosive. He noted Seeker's expression as he revealed the bomb. "You know this, too? Very good, sir, I'm glad we have a very clear understanding." The Talon moved to Anderson as the driver pulled her arms back to tie her hands with another piece of rope, and The Talon slowly unbuttoned her white blouse, the wet fabric easily revealing the Kevlar vest she wore underneath. He pulled the shirt open over both of Anderson's shoulders and began unstrapping the vest. Once the last Velcro strap was separated, he eased the vest off her torso, revealing her small, pert breasts. "Well, well, I am impressed by your very excellent physique, madam. Truly an exquisite American beauty." He stepped to the dumpster and tossed her vest in. Then he removed the Beretta's holster, her cell phone, and her FBI badge from her belt, tossing them in the trash. Without bothering to button up her blouse he ordered them all, "Get in the back of the truck, please."

CHAPTER 2

Seeker, Anderson, and Lizzy got into the pickup bed by sitting on the lowered gate and swiveling themselves in. The movement caused Anderson's blouse to fall completely to her wrists, leaving her topless with only her black slacks still on.

"Please lie down," The Talon said. After his hostages were on their backs, he ordered the driver to cover them with a large tarp which was lying in the truck bed against one side. The driver then weighted the corners down with toolboxes and full drywall mud pails. The trio under the tarp heard the front cabin doors open and the truck gently wobble back and forth, followed by the doors closing. "Drive on," they heard The Talon tell the driver.

Once the vehicle started moving Seeker said to Anderson, "Um, you wanna tell me why you don't have a bra on?"

She whispered through gritted teeth, "Because it's somewhere in your damn bedsheets. Or, did you forget we both got the call during coitus make-me-groan-us? Man, I am so billing you for my wardrobe and cheating me out of what was gonna be a great time."

"I didn't tell you to do a striptease while in hot pursuit, honey."

"Don't 'honey' me, mister. Right now, we're weaponless, tied up, and I'm too pissed to give a shit. I swear to God every time I get stuck in an assignment with you I end up bound and gagged. So, you got any great escape ideas?" She looked over at Lizzy beside her under the tarp. "Sorry, Lizzy, we're kinda being ourselves here. We'll get out of this." She looked back at Seeker. "Well, hero? Did your equally-mysterious boss fit you with any super secret gizmos?"

"Actually, yes." Seeker rolled away from Anderson so she could see his hands bound behind him. While the tarp blocked most of the sunlight, she could see that his elbow-high black gloves were swollen to nearly three times normal size. The ropes binding his wrists were stretching. He pressed his forefingers to the outsides of his thumbs, and his gloves immediately deflated to normal size with no evidence of ever having expanded. He easily slipped the tied ropes off his wrists.

"Nice trick," said Anderson.

He rolled back over toward her and reached into the lining of his left glove over the outer arm and pulled out a long flat-edge blade. In seconds he freed Anderson and Lizzy and removed Lizzy's gag. "Move slowly under me," he said to Anderson, who was lying between him and Lizzy. "Don't move the tarp any more than necessary."

It was easier to slip her arms out of her blouse than try to wiggle it back up over her shoulders. She slid herself under Seeker as he propped himself up on hands and toes just enough to give her room to move. "You say one word about how good this feels and I'll knee you right in the Johnsons," she said as she passed beneath him.

"Ha-ha, very funny, honey. It's not as if I planned to do a kidnap-rescue on my vacation here in Charleston. No offense, Lizzy."

"N-none taken?" she asked. She looked down at her stomach, afraid to move. "What about that?"

"Let's see about getting that off you," he said with a comforting smile. He reached into the other glove's lining and pulled out a narrow pouch. He opened the top cover to reveal several small jewelers' screwdrivers.

"Just how the hell do you have the right tools right when you need them?" Anderson asked.

As he started examining the explosive attached to Lizzy's stomach, he said, "Well, I could give you this long explanation of how my boss, The Spy, ran this long algorithm of the most common pieces of equipment the Task Force field agents use, and creating sets of miniature duplicates hidden in parts of our uniforms to use in case our primary set is not available for any reason."

"Ah, your fancy Batman utility belt."

"Actually, his is yellow. Didn't you ever watch the TV show?" He touched the rubber seal holding the bomb to her bare skin, the top edge over her belly button and the bottom edge just above where her pubic hair started under her panties. "Biological bonding agent. Very nice. Steph, I'm gonna need some solvent."

"Right! Let me get the Bat-biological bonding solvent from my Robin utility belt. Do I look like I have any solvent on me?"

"My boot, honey. Right heel. Pop it off and give me the contents."

She bent in half to grab his foot and pulled at his right boot heel until it came off in her hand, and said, "If the other is a phone, I'm gonna call you Maxwell Smart."

"Uh, it is a phone." He took the four small tubules she gave him from the right heel's hidden cavity. "Or rather, holds a phone in its own special air-tight, waterproof wrap." He gently broke the tops of the four tubules and dripped the contents one after the other along the entire seal of the explosive, while Anderson pushed his boot heel back into place. In less than a minute the seal detached and the device easily slid off her stomach and into his gloved hand. "OK, I'm gonna drop this out of the truck, so when we take down Talon it won't matter if he releases that dead man's switch or not. I'll take Talon, you take the driver."

"And why do you get the big bad?"

"I'm on the right side of the truck, maybe?"

"Oh, please…" They reached for the tarp corners and the blocks holding them down. "Lizzy," she said, "stay down best you can, now. It's gonna get real ugly real fast." Lizzy nodded silently and pushed back against the truck bed wall. Anderson and Seeker nodded at each other…

…and pulled the tarp free from its anchors. As one they leapt out of the truck bed and into the front of the truck cab through the open driver and passenger windows. As he moved, Seeker tossed the explosive as far away as he could. Anderson grabbed the driver's head and smashed it against the steering wheel. Pushing the unconscious driver aside, she got behind the steering wheel and used her toes to push the brake pedal to the floor, bringing the truck to a stop. She turned the engine off and put the key in her pocket.

As for The Talon…he was not there.

Anderson opened the driver's door and pulled the now-semi-conscious man out of the vehicle.

She stood over him and grabbed him by his shirtfront with both fists. He looked down at her bare breasts and smiled. "Hey, eyes up here, asshole," she said, pointing to her own eyes. He looked up, and the last thing he saw was her fist colliding with his face. She retrieved her Beretta from the unconscious driver's waistband.

A car passed them on the highway as Seeker came to her side with a zip tie from another secret pouch in his uniform and her blouse. The male driver honked his car horn at her, and Anderson just put her fists on her hips and cocked her head at him. She tied up the driver, and then accepted her shirt with a small smile. "Well, you always wanted to see me naked in the Lowcountry, what did you think?"

"I think you'd make a perfect calendar centerfold," Seeker answered, a big smile on his face. He looked around at the trees and the divided four-lane road. "Where are we?"

Anderson looked around. "Highway 17, south of Charleston, but still in Charleston County." She pointed at his boot with her recovered Beretta. "You mind making a call for backup?"

"What do we need backup for? We caught the henchman; we can drive back to the city and process him at your headquarters."

"What about The Talon? We heard him get in the truck, where'd he go?"

"He may have never been in the truck, just made us think he did. He's a wily one, The Talon. He's always one step ahead of everyone. Kind of amazing we were even given the chance to escape, never mind actually succeed. He doesn't make mistakes like that. But then, he didn't leave any of his hired help alive to testify... well, WE didn't leave any alive, dammit, except Sleeping Beauty over there," he said, pointing at the unconscious driver.

As a few more cars passed them, he dropped the truck bed gate and sat on it, inviting Lizzy by the hand to come forward and sit next to him. Anderson sat on her other side, gun pointed at the driver at all times. Lizzy collapsed against Seeker and hugged him, holding him tight, and shaking as she cried. "Lizzy, you're safe now. You're safe. We're sorry you had to be with him the last couple days, we only got word about you this morning when the ransom demand came through, and your father finally decided to contact the authorities. He was trying to get you back through his own efforts, they just weren't working. He never gave up on you, he just knew quickly he needed help. How are you doing? Did he do anything to you, touch you wrong?"

The teenager sat up, held her arms across her chest, holding her upper arms, still shivering from shock. "I'm ok," she said. "He didn't touch me, except for that bomb. I don't even know when he took me…I went to sleep in my bed, and woke up in some strange room, like magic. Who was he?"

"The Talon is an international extortionist, and kidnapper, and over-all bad dude, and aside from us no one has ever seen him face-to-face and lived. That's going to make a problem for you. Maybe some special protection service for a while." He crossed his left leg across his knee and removed the phone from its heel compartment. It was a small flip-phone, and there was no number pad, only one small button that he pressed. "Proteus, Seeker," he said.

A woman's voice came from the phone. "Proteus. What's up?"

He looked at Lizzy. "Ever consider switching to long blonde hair and a different eye color? You're gonna need to disappear for a while for your own protection," he told

Lizzy. To his phone he said, "Got a complete makeover for you to do."

CHAPTER 3

"I'm still not used to seeing you in a normal suit," Stephanie said. She was wearing a short one-piece black dress that displayed every bit of her long, smoothly muscled legs. She wore closed-toe pumps, her feet too scratched up for the strap heels she really wanted to wear for their date. "So, what's up with Lizzy?"

Calvin wore gray slacks, light blue shirt, and a dark blue sports coat with matching dark blue pants, and ankle-boots. He sported regular black sunglasses despite the growing darkness of sunset. "She's been moved to witness protection, with her father's consent. Proteus is our expert on disguise and camouflage, so no one will ever find Lizzy when she's done with the girl."

After their server brought their wine and glasses and poured their servings, he lifted his glass in toast. "To Special Agent Anderson, my gorgeous Southern FBI belle. Today was a great vacation day."

She lifted her glass in return. "To Task Force Agent Seeker, or whatever your real name is. You certainly know how to show a lady a good time like no one else." They clinked glasses and sipped at the same time. She shook her head, smiling. "I have no idea why I can never say 'no' to you. You're a pain in my ass."

He took another sip before setting down his own glass. "Because deep down you really love me?"

"Don't flatter yourself, Mister Agent. We have great sex, okay? Oh my, we have some REALLY great sex... But there ain't no 'love'." She smiled at him slyly; she really did love him.

He leaned forward. "Is there anyone else? Another man? A woman?"

"Oh, you wish... you'd love to see me with a woman, wouldn't you?"

"Can't say I wouldn't enjoy it," he said.

"Well, put it to rest, sweetheart. I'm a one-agent woman, even if all I know of you is you're part of a secret team with the hottest uniforms and incredible equipment and weapons. I don't know where you live, what your real name is, whether you're married and I'm just a fling whenever you're in Charleston. You've probably got special agent girlfriends in every city!" She took a long sip from her glassk and sighed, saying mostly to herself, "Hell, I can't believe I'm really in love with a superhero."

He shifted his chair so he could lean forward, closer to her. "I'm not a superhero, just a guy doing his job."

Without warning she threw a roundhouse that landed squarely on his chin, knocking him out of his chair and onto the carpet. The few other patrons of the restaurant dropped their silverware, the echoing clangs adding to the attention Stephanie did not notice. She got up and stood over him at his shoulders with her legs spread just enough for him to get a good view. "First of all, I owe you that. Second, you'll notice there is no underwear, Seeker, so if you wanna visit there again you gotta give me something… aside from a new suit and pair of shoes." She bent over slightly, extending a hand to help him to his feet.

Seeker accepted her hand and let her help him up. Once he was standing he suddenly wrapped his arms around her torso and kissed her hard, allowing her arms to move up around his neck when she stopped resisting. The restaurant patrons did not understand what was going on, but definitely preferred passion to punches while they tried to enjoy their own meals.

Their lips finally parted, and Anderson felt slightly woozy. "Dammit, I hate it when you do that," she growled softly. "Don't you dare do that again." He replied by pulling her back even harder and kissing her longer, and the restaurant patrons either watched and smiled or looked away, also smiling. A full minute later he eased her back into her seat and took his own. "OK," she said, "you talked me into it. Just get the whole bottle and we'll go to my place."

"Actually, we're going to my place."

CHAPTER 4

"Thanks for the tip, Hunter," Seeker said into his celphone as he drove his black Task Force car onto the exit ramp from Interstate-26 to go to the Charleston AFB/International Airport. His special Federal clearances allowed him to drive out to a 747 parked away from the main terminal. The aircraft was painted blue-gray underneath and black on top. While all the other number and letter markings looked standard, she noticed next to the front door behind the cockpit was the circle-in-a-circle emblem she remembered from his gun belt. "This is yours?" she asked, unable to hide the amazement in her voice.

"Yup," he said. "This is where I live."

"How the hell does a Task Force agent afford his own 747?"

"When one doesn't have a wife, one has extra disposable cash."

She scowled at him.

He drove past the rear of the aircraft and turned around to drive up the rear ramp into the belly of the craft. After he brought the car to a stop and turned off all the computer displays that replaced the normal dashboard gauges, he got out, went around the car, and opened the door for Anderson as the rear ramp rose and locked into place. He led her forward as lock bars rose from the floor and locked into place around the car's tires so the vehicle could not roll around while the plane was in flight. He stepped forward to a plasma-screen panel which flared to life when he pressed the bottom right corner. The video image was of the pilot at his post in the cockpit, a red-haired man with light freckling; Anderson figured the man to be in his 40s. "Lee, let's get this bird in the air."

"Roger, Seek. About ten minutes." The screen went blank.

"Hey, wait just one damn minute!" said Anderson. "Just what the hell do you think you're doing; you're kidnapping ME?"

"This isn't a kidnapping, honey," said Seeker. "My teammate Hunter got word of a possible sighting of The Talon in Buenos Aires, and I thought you might like a second crack at him."

"But I only have two days left on vacation!"

"Already taken care of. Your director gave you special dispensation to travel with me on this case, however long it takes."

"But I can't go tracking down a suspect like this! I gotta go home and pack some things, I can't be chasing a fugitive in a black dress miniskirt!"

"You did pretty good wearing only pants earlier today, letting the world see your very nice bosom without a second thought. Not to worry, I have a whole wardrobe available for you." He led her out of the car bay into the adjoining section, which was a galley with a spiral ladder going up to the next deck. At the top they turned right in the hallway looking out the starboard side of the plane and to the door at the end of the hall. He opened the door and stepped back so she could enter his master suite.

It filled the rear half of the top deck, a combined bedroom / living room / office complex. He showed her the closets at the rear which contained several of his standard black uniforms, sets of boots and gloves, several gun belts with his emblem in the flat metal buckle, more sets of cocoon glasses on a rear shelf, and a complete wardrobe of women's clothes in her exact size. There was a door in the far corner that led to the full bathroom. "Hum, looks like you thought of everything... almost. You expect me to chase a terrorist and beat him with my great charm? I have my gun and a spare mag, and that's it." She wiggled her purse in emphasis.

Seeker smiled and opened a side panel beside the closets. He introduced her to a retractable arsenal of handguns, rifles, and military armaments. She whistled as she eyed all the weaponry, pulled down a shiny Colt .357 from a shelf and smiled at him. "You can undo my zipper anytime, Agent Seeker," she said with a teasing grin.

He wrapped his arms around her and kissed her again, hard. She lifted her arms around his neck, and he felt the revolver rest against his shoulder blade as he slowly pulled the back zipper of her dress down until he reached the bottom of the zipper panel at the small of her back. The dress fell away and revealed she not only wore no panties but also no bra. Wearing only her black pumps she stepped slowly across the room, still carrying the empty revolver, and sat seductively on the edge of the bed, legs crossed at the knees. Seeker crossed the room to her and leaned down to kiss her.

After their lips parted she said in a soft voice, "I hate you, you son of a bitch."

He answered by leaning forward and kissing her neck, ears, and shoulders. She started by sliding his jacket off over his shoulders and pulling his shirt from his pants. While undoing the buttons she said in growing desire, "Oh, my God, I hate you so much!"

CHAPTER 5

Stephanie stepped out of the airplane's bathroom into the adjoining luxury bedroom. She wore only a white cotton thong and black high-heeled pumps; her sandy-blonde hair cascaded over her bare shoulders. Stepping into the dim bedroom, the light from the bathroom silhouetted her, and she seemed to glow like an angel. She kept one hand behind her back.

Seeker's talents as a Task Force agent included an extensive knowledge of international cultures, the ability to easily pick up new languages, and had his own vast network of contacts across the globe. His travels as Task Force Agent "Seeker" garnered him an incredible amount of financial support from people he aided over the years, creating a vast financial fortune from direct monetary gifts and skilled investments. This allowed him to purchase the 747, which he christened *The Adventure*, and retrofitted it as his home. All the furniture and equipment were bolted in place so it wouldn't move around while in flight. His jet had the full necessities of any home: bathrooms with showers, a living room, bedrooms, a kitchen, and a dining area on the main deck. The crew's quarters were in the forward area of the second deck. The public office areas had state-of-the-market equipment on the top deck, behind the cockpit. The cargo area underneath held his Task Force car along with food supplies and other necessities for the crew.

He very much enjoyed his domicile, watching Stephanie gradually approach the bed in which he lay.

Only a few steps from the bed she began a slow pirouette, finally raising her hand with a Colt .357. Hands behind his head, Seeker watched the show with increasing curiosity and an immediate arousal.

When she finished her spin, she pointed the gun at his chest. Seeker's eyebrows involuntarily rose and his hands fell to the bed.

She slowly crept onto the bed and straddled him atop the silk sheet. Stephanie placed the gun barrel on Seeker's throat and gave a sensuous smile.

Seeker felt the cold steel touch his skin; he narrowed his eyes and gave a slight grin. "Steph, I really like it when you get all kinky on me. Whatcha got in mind, beauty?"

Not answering, she deliberately dragged the tip of the gun down his chest, the sheet moving down with it, exposing tufts of black curly chest hair accentuated by light chocolate colored skin. "Sometimes—I like it just a little," she paused for emphasis, "rough, you know." She continued sliding the pistol down until it exposed a very nude and extremely stimulated Seeker.

"Oh, do you now?" Before she knew what was happening, Seeker reached for something beneath his pillow, grabbed it, and flipped Stephanie face down on the bed. He rose and straddled her bottom while he cuffed her hands behind her back. He removed the pistol from her hand, and deliberately slid it down her pearly white back. He laid his strong muscled body atop hers and whispered in her ear, "This what you had in mind, beauty?"

Stephanie turned her head and smiled big. "It'll do, for a start—"

A couple hours later, Stephanie sat back on the plush couch in the communications deck, behind *The Adventure*'s cockpit. She now wore a white blouse, blue-gray slacks, and simple black flats, and her outfit matched the steel-gray color of the couch's fabric. Her arms were crossed, and she stared at Seeker. "You're taking me to a place with jungles and snakes, aren't you?"

Seeker swiveled around in his chair. He was dressed in blue jeans, black western boots, and a gray T-shirt. "What snakes? What are you talking about, Steph?"

"Argentina, it's full of tarantulas, insects, and man-eating ants. How can I protect myself from that? You want me to shoot at a bug every time one flies up in front of me? Besides, why would The Talon flee to a jungle anyway?"

Seeker smiled and swiveled back to his computer station. He was amused with her lack of knowledge about the foreign country. He did a quick computer search, turned back around, and waved a hand at the computer screen. "See? No jungles in the city. If you'll notice, it's a big city, not unlike Charleston or any other big city you've been to. Buenos Aires literally means 'fair winds'. It's the capital of the country. It's got buildings, houses, landscaping, fountains, a huge ass harbor, regular people…who happen to just speak Spanish, instead of Southern."

"Ha, ha," Stephanie said, not amused.

Seeker leaned forward, resting his arms on his knees. "Unless you want me to find us a jungle over there? I'll be Tarzan, you Jane. We'll see what kind of snake we can find out there for you." Seeker grinned.

Stephanie felt dumb for her ignorance of the place. Of all the places she'd ever been, this is one she'd never studied about or been to. "Oh, shut up, Seeker."

Seeker turned back around, continuing his research on The Talon, his gang, legal records, and anywhere he might be hiding out in the big city. "Quit pouting and get your ass over to this other computer and help me do some research. We've got cyber investigating to do on The Talon and his accomplices, and only have a few hours before we land."

"Yeah, OK. Lemme go use the restroom first then I'll come back and help you. Suppose it's the least I could do." Stephanie headed to the forward restrooms.

"Hope everything comes out alright!" Seeker bellowed, without looking up from his screen.

"Screw you, Seeker."

"You wish," he retorted. "I know you dream about me!" he shouted, and grinned at their ongoing banter.

When Stephanie returned, one of Seeker's staff occupied the seat and terminal to his left. Her back was to Stephanie and was already busy on the computer. She heard Stephanie approach and rose to introduce herself.

"Ms. Anderson, pleased to meet you. I am Mr. Geffers' personal aid," the woman spoke with assured confidence. Her glasses sat low on her nose. Her tone was deep, almost that of a man's voice, and with a slight accent, which Stephanie couldn't place, *almost British*, she thought.

The woman clutched her hands behind her back, held her chin up, and stated with authority, "I am Ms. Murphy. My duties are to assist Mr. Geffers with investigations, research, computer programming, language translation, procurement, encryption decoding, and any other such duties as required. I'm fifty-five years old, and I hold black belts in numerous martial arts." Ms. Murphy returned to her computer terminal, sat, and continued her research.

Stephanie whispered aloud, "Wow. What an introduction."

Seeker stood up, walked over to her, and gave her a gentle, lingering kiss. "Calm down, my beauty. That's just a tidbit of what I'm gonna give you in the hotel room tonight."

Seeker's kiss did calm her down, it always did. She looked up at his seductive green eyes. "You know, you have a bedroom in your plane, we were in it a while ago." Whispering in his ear she said, "We could join the Mile High Club again, this time in the Southern Hemisphere."

"Who says I haven't already?" Seeker said, smiling.

She slugged him with a roundhouse-right. Ms. Murphy's head turned slightly, not wanting to miss a good fight.

He rubbed his jaw with his hand. "OK, I deserved that." He reached forward and took Stephanie's hand and led her to the computer station to his right. "Come on, little bulldog, let's get some work done."

She gazed over at his aid. Stephanie sighed and took her seat. "What else have I got to do for the next few hours anyway?"

"Atta girl. And by the way, her daughter Sam is our chef on board." Stephanie raised her eyebrows, considering the thought of two "Ms. Murphys" aboard the jet.

"Her daughter was fresh out of culinary school and both looking for work, so I hired 'em," he explained. "Come on, I need you to look up the American Embassy in Buenos Aires, give 'em a call. Verify that the Embassy's protocols are still up to date and give them a head's up on our arrival. I gotta call the boss. We took off so quick, I forgot to even call in and give an update on what was my vacation. He'll have my ass," he said as he picked up the phone receiver on the desk beside his computer.

Stephanie said under her breath, "No, I get your ass next."

The three typed, researched, and studied during the long flight. They reviewed Interpol records, attempting to learn more about The Talon and his allusive associates around the world. They got a semi-full dossier on the man and his travels as was possible; finding out that he was a very clever and astute criminal.

Stephanie reported to Seeker, "Looks like we're all ready. Embassy personnel are going to meet us at the airport and take us where we need to go; got full cooperation."

Lee the pilot called from the cockpit over the plane's audio system. "Seeker? We're landing in about fifteen. Got priority clearance. Just lettin' you know their security will be waiting on the runway with a vehicle for you and Agent Anderson to go to the Embassy. Please prepare for descent."

Pressing a speaker button on the console, he stated, "Yep, doing that right now." Seeker printed off the paperwork he needed and placed it inside a briefcase. He instructed the two ladies to follow him to a seating area forward of the living room. "Buckle up, ladies; this will be a smooth landing as usual."

The Adventure gently landed on the tarmac in the clear night-time, and the force of the brakes made everyone lean forward slightly as the plane wheeled to its parking location. Ms. Murphy unbuckled quickly and assumed her position at the exit door near the flight deck. Once the jet came to a complete stop, she unlocked the door and waited for the rolling staircase to arrive. Three Argentinian security agents immediately climbed the steps to enter the plane. One stepped forward; he wore a dark gray suit, black tie and shoes, white shirt, and his graying black hair was brushed back from his balding pate. His dark brown eyes were anything but friendly, and his tall slim frame looked ready to attack.

Ms. Murphy stopped the agent in front at the plane's entrance; he looked down at her while he tried to step around her, but she remained in his path. "Move aside, woman," he sneered at her in a thick Spanish accent.

She narrowed her eyes at him. "You're welcome to try moving me."

The agent continued glaring at her, eye-to-eye, and then finally smiled. "I like you, Ms. Murphy. It's good to see you again."

Ms. Murphy returned his smile and extended her hand in greeting. "Good to see you, too, Leon."

Seeker and Stephanie arrived at the front exit. Seeker shook Leon's hand. "Hello, old friend," he said.

"Ah, Seeker, very nice to have you back in Argentina. You do remember protocol requires you to let me inspect your jet." Seeker waved his hand to someone behind him in the plane, and Ms. Murphy's daughter, Miss Murphy, stepped forward holding a small box.

They could be twins, thought Stephanie upon seeing the mother-daughter duo together for the first time.

Miss Murphy handed the box to Seeker; he opened it and showed Leon its contents. Leon smiled and Seeker closed it. Leon took the box in his arms, and said, "Once again, your plane is clean and authorized to park in Buenos Aires. Just remember to keep your armaments out of sight while visiting our beautiful city." He shook Seeker's hand, turned around, and waved his fellow agents to go down the stairs.

"What the hell was that?" Stephanie asked.

"Better that you don't know," Seeker said. He looked down at his black Task Force uniform and adjusted his gun belt with its equipment pouches attached around its circumference. "Ms. Murphy, please see to the hotel arrangements for Agent Anderson and me and anyone who wants to get off *The Adventure* for a bit, while we go to the Embassy. Oh, and make sure to grab our luggage." He took Stephanie's hand in his and led her down the stairs to the waiting black SUV.

There was an Embassy agent standing beside the back door of the car, dressed in a standard black suit, black glasses, and slicked-back dark-brown hair. Seeker and Stephanie approached and the agent stopped them. "No weapons," said the agent, eyeing Seeker's gun belt.

Seeker looked at the man, amused at his authoritative demeanor. "You must be new," said Seeker to the Argentinian agent. "Radio your supervisor for verification code TFAS1, protocol Intercept, authorization Sugar Cane."

"That is not a valid authorization code." He reached for his gun in his shoulder holster.

Before the agent could slip his fingers inside his suit coat, Seeker had already drawn his weapon and pointed it at the agent's forehead. "Stop trying to impress my lady friend. That code is valid for five minutes only, and we've used up four of 'em getting to this point. Just make the call, junior."

The embassy agent eyed Seeker, contemplating an action. He finally spoke into his cuff microphone.

Stephanie whispered into Seeker's ear, "'Sugar Cane'?"

The agent dropped his hand and looked at Seeker, and visibly swallowed hard. He stood straight and opened the back door of the SUV. "My apologies, sir. Please get in."

The couple got in the rear seat and the agent closed the door. When the SUV began moving, Seeker relaxed and crossed his legs.

"Wow, if I hadn't seen all this I wouldn't have believed it," Stephanie said, giving an exaggerated swing of both arms.

"Believe what?" Seeker asked.

"The past day! My God, I still can't believe I let you pick me up on vacation back home, and we started having sex *again* on the first night, then the call about the kidnapped girl, and one of your secret agents telling you the girl was seen at a Charleston dock. Who do we see there? The Talon! Interpol's number one wanted criminal! We end up in a gunfight, you blow up the dock, we get caught by The Talon, I get stripped half-naked and thrown in a truck with you and the kidnapped girl. Then we escape, and your secret agent friends inform you they tailed Talon and he was on his way to Buenos Aires. Then we're in your plane, I had no idea you had your own big-ass plane! Just how rich are you, anyway? This whole twenty-four hours has been something out of a James Bond movie."

The agents in the front seat overheard the lengthy, almost heated one-sided conversation. The driver looked in the rear-view mirror to watch the two and smiled. The two men said something to each other in Spanish, entertained by Stephanie's ramblings. From the conversation, the men assumed the two were married.

"And next thing I know we're flying here. You didn't give me a chance to pack my clothes or get my toothbrush, of course I find out you've already bought me a whole wardrobe and toothbrush, and then I find out you have your own staff!" She leaned close to him and pointed a finger, whispering, "But I finally learned something important about you, Mr. Secret Agent Seeker; your last name is Geffers!"

Seeker looked at her. "Is it?"

Stephanie stared at his eyes. "Oh, don't you tell me that's a cover name. I've earned the right to know your real name after all the times," she paused, her scowl precipitatedly turned into a grin. She looked at Seeker, top to foot, admiring his physique and realizing, again, how handsome he was. Her mind temporarily wandered off to how passionate their sex together was. "After all the times I've let you between my legs…and, oh my God," she lowered her voice, "you're so good there."

Seeker looked over at Stephanie and smiled at her after her long-winded dialog. Streetlights illuminated her face while they drove. "You're beautiful, Steph. You have no idea how much I love you, you know; you're the most awesome woman I've ever met."

Cooled down, Stephanie leaned in hard against Seeker, pulling him close to place a delicate kiss on his lips. There was no doubt she found him tantalizing, and at this point irresistible. Seeker kissed back, determined, holding her luscious hair in his hands.

The sudden silence from the back seat aroused the attention of the guard in the passenger seat. Turning his head slightly, he saw the couple kissing, Stephanie stretching hard toward Seeker, forcing her blouse up and bare midriff skin was revealed. The guard grinned but did a double take when he saw the .357 in a black holster on her hip. He said something to the driver in Spanish, and both gave a hearty laugh.

Barely moving from Seekers lips, she listened to the snickers from the front seat. Stephanie asked, "Wonder what's up?"

Seeker barely heard her words, too caught up in the moment. "Chemistry, baby. Chemistry."

The SUV came to a stop at the back gate of the Embassy. Two security guards stood at their posts, one on either side of the security gate. One approached the driver's window, and a conversation ensued between the guard and the driver.

In the back seat, Stephanie spoke up. "Seeker, I know that's Spanish, but there's a lot I don't understand."

"Yeah, there's a bunch of Spanish dialects here, Steph. There's also a bunch of other nationalities that live here that speak their own native language. Like Italian, Arabic, German, and so on. Since Our Talon is German, and there's right at one million Germans residing here, that's most likely the people he's hanging out with."

Stephanie listened intently. "Sounds like he's asking if we had an appointment with the FBU, Seeker. What's FBU? The embassy person I spoke with earlier said there was no problem."

"Federal Benefits Unit." Seeker answered. "Yeah, normally people would need to make an appointment to get in, but our driver here is explaining what we're doing. It'll be fi—"

Seeker was cut short when the driver announced to the two agents that they were being let in. The security gate opened and the SUV proceeded into a secure underground parking garage. Both were escorted into an elevator and one of the security guards punched the number five button.

"I had no idea this place was so big, Seeker."

"Yeah, pretty impressive."

"You've been here before?"

"A time or two."

Stephanie shrugged her shoulders. "I shoulda known."

The elevator came to a stop and the doors opened. The two were led down a hallway and into a conference room where two male American agents were awaiting their arrival. The agents stood when Seeker and Stephanie entered. They all exchanged greetings and finally sat to hear Seeker's mission in Argentina.

"We were to report our arrival to the Ambassador," Seeker finally said after explaining his and Stephanie's encounter with The Talon.

"We've already taken care of that for you, sir. When Agent Anderson here," said one agent, pointing at Stephanie, "called in, we advised the Ambassador, and he gave us instructions to help you and give full cooperation."

Seeker answered, "We've gotten a few more intel leads since leaving Charleston. The unknown, however, is where he is right now and how many he's hired to work for him here. This is also the closest anyone's ever come to catching him. We can use all the help we can get."

CHAPTER 6

Thirty-seven-year-old Mark Jason, president of Jason Enterprises, looked up from the financial reports on his desktop computer. His assistant, Eleanor Worthington entered, from her adjoining office, crossed his expansive workplace past the furnished conversation area, and the wet bar on the far wall. She walked with the prim, proper stature, and etiquette of her strict English upbringing. Eleanor always wore her blonde hair back in a tight, severe bun. Mark had no idea how long her hair truly was, despite the years she'd worked for him.

She came to a stop at his desk and stood smartly with a portfolio crossed in her arms. "Yes, Ellie?" he asked, using her nickname that no one else dared use in her presence.

"The report from Program 12-AC79 on the 14th floor," she replied calmly. Her English accent made her voice flow like an endless melody.

"Save me the time," Mark said, leaning back in his executive chair. "Pass or fail?"

She removed her eyeglasses and let them dangle on her chest by the 14 carat gold chain. Eleanor gave one of her rare emotional responses; she closed her eyes and lowered her jaw slightly. "Fail, sir, I'm afraid. The J-9X module crashed on the final test." Eleanor hated reporting bad news to Mark.

Mark rubbed his cheeks in frustration, the posture making his heavily muscled arms tighten the fabric of his suit coat around his biceps. When he brought his hands back down his dark brown beard hairs stood straight up. "OK, this has *got* to be fixed. Call Hito and tell him to shorten his vacation. We're already pushing the deadline on this new laser infrared guidance system, and the Joint Chiefs want this in the new rockets for fighting Al-Qaida. *If* the president will stiffen his spine and let 'em use it. If Hito can get this shit fixed within the week, I'll make sure he gets double time off at Christmas…on me."

"I already called him with that offer, sir, and he'll be in the office tomorrow morning."

Mark looked up at her stoic face. "Should I be surprised that I've become that predictable, Ellie?"

"Not predictable, sir," she said. "It was the only logical next step to keep the admiral off your ass."

"Indeed," he said, his eyebrows raised in response to her forward answer. Mark leaned forward over his desk, reached up and retrieved the portfolio from her. He took a moment to glance over the summary pages before initialing the bottom of the front page. "Well, my ass and I thank you for your consideration of this plight. If the admiral calls—"

Interrupting his sentence, Eleanor replied in a low slow monotone, "You are unavailable while you're figuring out his pain in your ass."

"I do like your official terminology," Mark said with a smile.

"By the way sir, your 2:30 review is here." Eleanor added.

"Ah, yes, our intern with the happy supervisor," Mark said as he glanced at the flashing reminder on his computer terminal. "Send them in, please, Ellie."

"Yes, sir." Eleanor turned on her heel, proceeded to the interoffice door, and opened it, asking the two women to enter.

Both women wore white lab coats over their civilian attire: formal, bland skirts and flat shoes. The supervisor, Annette Penning, was slightly overweight and prematurely gray but still attractive, and only a couple inches shorter than the six-foot-four company president. Her intern, Crystal Leigh, was five-foot-two with dark brown hair pulled back in a loose ponytail and wore dark Franklin-style glasses. Mark watched the pair enter his office, and couldn't help but form a small grin, thinking the two appeared almost *too* scientific, *too* nerdy.

Mark rose from his chair and extended his hand to Annette first. "Good to see you again, Annette," he said, smiling. He then greeted young Crystal. "Pleased to see you again, too, Crystal, I've been hearing good things about you."

"It's a great honor to meet you again, Mr. Jason," Crystal said, accepting his hand and giving a nervous, large smile; and suddenly she felt stupid for the exaggerated grin and lowered her eyes to the floor momentarily.

"Please have a seat, ladies." Mark waved at the two chairs across from him in invitation. Annette handed forward a binder to Mark as she sat. He accepted it and opened the cover, speed-reading the first page, then reclining back as he turned to page two and then three.

Annette sat in comfortable silence while Mark read the report. She was used to such meetings and the long waits while Mark perused through such files. Crystal, however, was quite uncomfortable in the extended silence, not yet accustomed to the corporate etiquette or protocols at Jason Enterprises. She jumped in her seat when Mark suddenly whistled. He sat forward in his chair, leaning hard against the desk, and stared at the intern intently. "*You* developed this?" he asked, more demanding than he intended.

Crystal's eyes searched the room for an answer. Blushing, she nervously answered, "Yes, sir."

"Has this been tested?" Mark asked Annette.

"First-level, Mr. Jason. One hundred percent results in the cultures. We normally need a long permit process from the FDA, the CDC, and the World Health Organization to go to the second level, but we've never had a hundred percent affirmation in the first-level tests before. It's unheard of. Crystal here did quite a job on this, sir."

More silence filled the office suite as Mark adjusted his reading glasses and read deeper into the report's pages. Crystal listened as the sound of the turning pages echoed throughout the room. "You designed this antitoxin yourself?" he asked Crystal again without looking up.

"Yes, sir," she answered, her voice still quivering. She couldn't help but feel the awe of sitting in front of one of the most powerful men in Richmond, Virginia. She knew he was a man, by reputation, who could break the will of any politician in Washington, D.C. "It's been a study of mine since I was a little girl—"

Mark held up a hand, interrupting her answer. "I wasn't ready for the personal history just yet," he said, the kindness in his voice in total opposition to the words. "That's a couple questions down the review process here."

"Yes, sir." Crystal nodded, shoving her hands between her knees. She wasn't sure if she should be embarrassed or feel complimented. He was exactly like his reputation. Firm, but always courteous.

"How long has she been assigned to this?" Mark asked Annette.

"This was not on her assigned duties. She did this entirely on her own time, Mr. Jason."

Mark turned his gaze to Crystal again, looking at her over the top of his glasses, this time with a more probing stare and mouth half open. "This antitoxin design, it's years ahead of even current military study and testing. Using a cross-species convergence of venom within a single genus, and then a universal toxin with no side-effects? Now, this is the personal question, Crystal. If you came up with this on your own time, why?"

Crystal dropped her head momentarily, and then looked up as she answered. "My younger brother, sir—he died from a bite—"

A cell phone abruptly rang in a dual-beep tone. Mark held his hand up, and momentarily closed his eyes while he reached into his inside jacket pocket. He recognized the phone number on the digital display and realized the importance of the call. "My apologies, ladies," he said as he stood. "Please remain seated, this should only take a moment." He stepped out from behind his desk and walked several steps over to the conversation area of his office. He opened the flip phone and said softly, "Go."

On the other end of the line was the voice of Task Force Agent Seeker. "Hope this isn't a bad time, boss," said the strong male voice.

"I always like being interrupted in the middle of an important break-through, agent," Mark whispered. "Update, and it needs to be the news I was waiting to hear since your call from the plane."

"I've followed The Talon to Buenos Aires. Checked in with the embassy, so if I kill anyone no one will get pissed off any more than necessary. Helluva vacation, boss."

"Always helps to be in the right place at the right time," Mark answered. He stood with his back to the women, his hand on his hip as he spoke. "Wait, what did you say? *Buenos Aires?* I don't remember signing a requisition for a Task Force jet to Buenos Aires for a four-thousand-mile trip!"

Mark's whisper turned into a growl; louder than he intended. Both women turned their heads in his direction.

"No boss, my personal jet, the 747."

"Oh, yeah, your home with wings. So, if you're off chasing our extortionist in some foreign country, what happened to the girl he kidnapped?"

"Got her, sir, just in time, too. She's fine and back with her parents. Proteus is preparing her for witness protection. Talon just slipped away. Hunter and the other agents forwarded intel that showed he fled to Buenos Aires, his home away from home."

Mark took a moment to process the information and let it roll around in his head. He'd read the criminal files when Seeker notified him when his trip south began, recalling what little was known of the international extortionist who was known only as "The Talon."

On the phone, Mark heard an unexpected female voice in the background. "Where the hell is my damn bra this time?" she shouted in an angry tone.

Mark closed his eyes and lowered his head. "Do I want to know what that's all about, Seeker?"

"Um, probably not, sir." Seeker stared at the naked woman ransacking his bed as he spoke with his superior. "I'll fill in all the details in my mission brief when I get back. I'd really like to get this guy, boss. And frankly he's pissed off Stephanie, too."

Mark stared at the wall. "Stephanie? As in FBI Special Agent Stephanie Anderson?"

"Um," the voice on the phone hesitated in reply. "Well, you could kinda say she got pulled into the case…as I said, I was on vacation."

Her voice interrupted from the background again. "I'm *not* wearing my thong on the hunt; I want my regular undies. Where did you pack them, Seeker?"

"Steph, shush—I'm on a call with the boss!"

Mark closed his eyes again. "Please, just don't let her make an international incident. And I definitely want regular reports on what's going on down there, no bras or thongs involved, please."

"Yes, sir," Seeker said, and the line went dead.

Mark tucked the phone back in his pocket and returned to his desk chair. "My apologies," Mark said with a half-hearted smile. "Just another one of those little international matters this company has to deal with on a regular basis. So, where were we? Ah, yes, Crystal. Give me a little more detail about how you arrived at this, um, formula."

Mark listened to the impressive young intern as she gave her formulaic dissertation of her findings, introspection, hypothesis, and final proven conclusions to her experiments.

He shuffled the papers into the folder and straightened them all. "Well, you've been an intern with us for six months now; I've read every single lab experiment you've worked on, talked with your supervisor here," pointing at Annette, and now this." He held up the folder. "I've never seen the likes of you young lady. Psychological testing, high IQ, the highest GPA possible, what can I say? You're damned near perfect. Someday, I hope to have you on my staff permanently. For now, I'm increasing your intern status to level nine. Trust me, you can go far with this company." Mark scribbled something on a notepad and passed it to Crystal. "And here's your new salary for the extent of your internship here while you're working on your PhD."

Annette got a big grin on her face and Crystal's face turned a bright pink.

"Mr. Jason, I-I don't know what to say. Thank you."

"No, thank *you*, Crystal. You may not realize what you've just done here in this particular experiment. The next thing we have to do is call some very important people. Then make a call to the US Patent and Trademark Office…"

CHAPTER 7

"All I can find to wear are thongs and lace bras!" Exasperated, Stephanie groaned as she sat on the tossed bed sheets in their Buenos Aires hotel room. "While I appreciate the wardrobe you had for me in your fancy flying house, I'd really rather be wearing normal underwear if I'm going to be shooting people. Thongs and cute little bows don't match bullets, ya know." Seeker sat in one of the hotel suite's plush armchairs and looked at her. He enjoyed looking at her wearing nothing more than a frustrated pout. He gazed at her pink-polished toes, then up to her neatly trimmed pubic strip, then to her small pert breasts, and finally at her intoxicating doe eyes. Stephanie's long sandy blonde hair hung un-brushed over her face and shoulders. "Next time you want to drag me out of the country, let me pack my own clothes, ok? Dammit!"

Seeker smiled at last and said, "Bottom drawer of the nightstand," he pointed to her left. She got up and went to the nightstand, bending over and giving Seeker an unplanned full view of her rear assets. "Oh, momma, so very nice," he said under his breath.

She stood up and turned to glare at him with her blue eyes. "You are not having a return trip to these goodies until we get this son of a bitch," she said. "God, I can't believe we had sex twice in a week! Why do I let you do that to me? And why do I like it so much?"

Seeker adjusted his elbow-high leather gloves, checking that all the miniature equipment was in place in the special seam pockets. "Chemistry," he said, smiling.

Stephanie pulled her white panties on, realizing just then that they, too, were thong-style as they slid into her butt crack. "Oh, please, are these the only kinda panties you bought me?"

He reached into a black bag beside his chair and removed a pink-trimmed Smith and Wesson 9MM handgun. "Was hoping you'd like this a little better." Smiling, Stephanie took the handgun and looked at it carefully, then tested its feel in her hand. "I had it custom-fit for you," he said. "And pink, just like you've been wanting."

"And just how did you manage that?" she asked. "No, never mind, thank you, Seeker, it's magnificent!" She looked in the bag. "No holster?"

"Just stick it in the back of your pants," said Seeker. "Well, could I interest you in dinner?"

"I'm gonna need a new outfit, Mister Seeker."

"Not a problem. There's a whole host of stores on the first floor of the hotel. I think we can find you something, appropriate."

Seeker and Stephanie strolled up the cobblestone sidewalk, on the ancient rickety rocks. He held Stephanie's arm to keep her from toppling over. "Note to self," Stephanie said, "never wear high heels on cobblestone. You think I'd know that after growing up in Charleston. Why the hell would anyone else build cobblestone streets?" She wobbled and stumbled her way, looking as if she had already had too much to drink.

"I gotcha, my beauty, just hang on to my arm. But, hey, it was your idea to wear the stilettos."

"They matched the new skirt! We're on a date, remember? It's my job to make you look good by looking even better than you. And flats don't do the job, boyfriend."

"And you're the hottest date I've ever had the pleasure of, um, escorting down the street."

They slowed and approached the restaurant. The entrance had two oversized wooden doors, gas-fueled sconces on the wall to the side of each; it gave an atmosphere of a medieval building. "It was a home built in the 1800s and turned into a restaurant many years ago. You like?"

"I like very much, Seeker, it's beautiful."

Stephanie slowed to look up at the restaurant's name above the door entrance. "'La Vache Française.'" What's that mean?"

"Ah, just something a little bullish. Nothing to worry about, I'll explain later." Seeker gave her a mystifying grin.

Once inside, the beauty of the place was breathtaking, and the smells of fresh baked bread lingered in the air. Candles on the tables lit the restaurant as did the gas flamed sconces on the walls, miniature versions of the ones outside. It had an old-world feel about it, with its aged wooden floors, French-style tapestries, decorative black security bars on the windows, and original paintings hanging from the walls that displayed portraits of men and women in the nude.

The maîtres d' looked up from his station when the two came in. In a heavy French accent, he greeted the couple, "Ah Monsieur Cherchuer and Mademoiselle Anderson. Welcome, welcome!" Moving from behind his desk, he took Stephanie's hand in his. "You are more magnificent than the Monsieur described you. His words gave no justice to your magnificent beauty, if I am permitted," he said as he brought her hand up with his and delicately placed a kiss on it.

"Hey, for once she's speechless," Seeker ribbed. "And if you kiss me, I'll slug you one."

The maître d' stood straight and extended his hand to Seeker. "Monsieur, it is nice to see you are in good spirits." Seeker shook his hand, palming a one-hundred-dollar bill for the man.

"Good to see you again, Olivier. I'll be in better spirits as soon as you see that we get some champagne. Never know when one might celebrate something." He winked at Stephanie, who gave him a strange look.

Olivier grabbed some menus from his desk, "Follow me if you would, I presume you'd like your favorite table Monsieur?"

"Yes, please." They followed along behind the maître d', noticing there was a large crowd and that the place hummed with chitchat.

"Celebrate what, Seeker?" Stephanie whispered. "We're not celebrating anything. We haven't even got The Talon yet."

"Hey, no worries. Don't have to have a special occasion to celebrate," he grinned as they walked. He gently patted at the small box in his jacket pocket.

Seeker preferred the table closest to the kitchen doors. The military/law enforcement part of his brain always told him to never sit with his back to a crowd, and to always have a quick escape route.

Arriving at the table, the maître d' motioned them to take a seat. Stephanie also knew the rule of thumb to not sit with one's back to a crowd. She ended up beside Seeker, both their backs facing the wall.

"Same champagne as always, Monsieur?"

"Yes," Seeker answered. "No sense in changing up a good thing now is there, Olivier?"

Placing the menus on the table, he replied, "Mais, non! Moreover, may I add that we have several fine entrees and exquisite appetizers for you this evening. Your waiter will be with you in a moment and that champagne is on its way. Please enjoy your meal, and you know where to find me should you need anything." Slightly bowing, the maître d' said, "Good to see you again, Monsieur, and nice to finally meet you, Mademoiselle."

Stephanie asked suspiciously, "What was all that about, Seeker? Champagne, several good things for tonight? Good to see you again? *And you've been here before?* Just what's up?"

"Nothin' baby, just trying to show you a good time. I come here often, OK? On business usually, or sometimes on my time off. You relax and enjoy the ambiance of this place, you'll like it." He patted her on the knee.

At that moment, the hostess arrived with their bottle of champagne, presented forward for inspection. Your "Champagne, sir, ma'am," she said in a distinctly Southern American accent.

"Hey, you're a southern girl?" Seeker said to her cheerily.

"Yes, sir. Afraid no French accent for this here girl. Georgia to be specific, sir. Down here on a student exchange program, just earning a little extra spending money. Anyways, Dom Perignon Rose? May I?" she said, asking permission to open the bottle.

"By all means, open and pour away. Keep another on hand just in case." Seeker winked at the hostess, who grinned back at him, making Stephanie crinkle her eyebrows again.

Seeker raised his glass to make a toast, Stephanie following suit. "To my beauty, the one I adore and would gladly travel the world with forever and ever."

Stephanie smiled, giving in to the mystery and resigned to have a good time as Seeker had suggested.

A man wearing a large fedora entered the restaurant alone and spoke with the maître d'. The man pointed to a table in the far corner opposite Seeker and Stephanie, and both headed in that direction.

As they walked, the man courteously nodded at a few of the patrons and spoke to a few others, telling them to enjoy their meal. Most greeted him back, as if they knew him. While he looked about, his eyes fell on the couple near the kitchen doors, both sitting close to one another, the man gently kissing the woman's neck.

"If you don't mind," the gentleman said, "I see some old friends. And I think I'd prefer to sit with them," pointing to Seeker and Stephanie.

"Of course, Monsieur, as you please."

Arriving at the table, the older gentleman pulled back a chair, and it gently scraped on the wooden floors as he removed his hat. Stephanie looked up at a man's green, twinkling eyes; Seeker was about to protest the man's uninvited arrival when he said in his soft, German accent, "Well, what an unexpected pleasure to see you again. You won't mind if I join you for a glass of wine, perhaps dinner even, yes?"

Seeker's demeanor abruptly went from content to fight mode. Stephanie reached for the new, pink gun, tucked into the back of her skirt as Seeker reached for one of the two guns tucked inside his jacket.

The Talon held up his hand. "No, keep your hands in sight, please, no need for any violence. Just look around, please."

Instinctively Seeker and Stephanie both glanced around as prompted, suddenly aware of the hush that fell silent within the restaurant. Most of the patrons had stopped their conversations and turned to face the three, all stone-faced. The Talon made himself comfortable, intertwining his fingers atop the table.

"You know, I have many, shall we say, friends in the restaurant with us. They go wherever I plan to go, you see, always in advance, of course."

Seeker turned and stared at Talon. His forehead furrowed, now realizing that most of the patrons were The Talon's crew. He instinctively put a hand on Stephanie's arm. Seeker replied through gritted teeth, "By all means, join us."

The Talon clicked his tongue on his teeth. "Oh, there's no reason to be so crass now. I'm here to join you for dinner, and a bit of pleasant conversation, that's all. You wouldn't deny me that, would you? These people," he said as he waved a hand outward, "are here to help, to protect me, you understand? It is so nice to see my old friends once again, yes? When I left you in Charleston, I had no idea that you managed to escape. And now, you are here in Buenos Aires. Bravo, well done. I am impressed that someone once again has found me. That has never happened before, but now you've managed to find me twice. I am duly impressed."

A waitress entered the restaurant through the kitchen doors, recognizing the German man right away and rushed to the table. She knew he spent a great amount of money in the restaurant, and even better, left huge tips. "Geehrter Herr, sehr ist es gut, Sie wieder zu sehen. Haben Sie Ihren üblichen Wein?"

The Talon looked up when the waitress spoke, recognizing her French accent, though she spoke to him in German. "Oh, my dear girl. I appreciate your wonderful knowledge of the German language. However, as I'm with my English-speaking friends, perhaps we can speak in their dialect so as not to confuse anyone."

"Yes, Geehrter Herr, I apologize. I saw you over here and wanted to make sure you were attended to. Would you prefer the special wine we keep in stock for you, or join in champagne with the lovely couple?"

"Yes, you are very astute my dear and I thank you for your attentiveness. Yes, the Dom Romane Conti 1997 would be wonderful." The Talon looked over at Seeker and Stephanie. "Are you familiar with this wine?"

Seeker's face was hard, cold and all his courtesy and manners had long passed. "Yes, indeed I am, Talon. Over a thousand dollars a bottle, the last time I checked."

The Talon leaned forward and whispered, "We shall have our wine, have our dinner, and no violence, until after dessert, please." He sat straight, hands on the table, fingers intertwined.

Stephanie whispered, "Seeker? What do we do?"

Seeker sat straight as well, well aware of how many guns and weapons were against them both. Finally, he said to The Talon, "Why don't we order dinner, sir, and discuss our situation."

"Ah, very wise, sir, very wise," said The Talon.

The appetizer course preceded quietly, no one speaking while sampling the crudités.

Seeker kept squeezing Stephanie's hand whenever he noticed her about to say something. He anticipated anything would ignite their volatile atmosphere.

When the appetizer plates were removed, The Talon said gently, "Well, I must know just how you escaped Charleston. Perhaps it was so remarkably simple, just having my driver take you into the woods outside the city to kill all three of you and bury your bodies. I didn't realize your resourcefulness."

"Trade secrets," Seeker said just as gently.

"Speaking of secrets," Talon continued, "you, my dear, are Special Agent Anderson." Her eyes widened when he said her name. "I saw your name on your badge when I disarmed you and removed your identification. But you, sir, you intrigue me; I can find nothing about you."

"You may call me Chercheur."

Talon raised an eyebrow, and then nodded politely. "Well, Monsieur Chercheur, I now know your nom de voyage. And I also know it's time for the salad. Service, si vous plais." On cue the first waitress came forward with a tray carrying three Caesar salads, serving Stephanie, Seeker, and Talon in order. She departed wordlessly, and Talon continued. "Well, then, I suppose that your escape will remain a mystery. Fine. So, as we continue our fine meal, I will share that you will remain alive to at least the end of dessert." That caused Stephanie's mouth to drop, while Seeker's expression remained neutral. "Oh, my dear, this is truly just business. I have succeeded by remaining unknown. But you and your lover here have crossed paths with me twice, and that is twice too many. So, my friends also dining here will dispatch you permanently, once our meal has concluded and I have departed."

Seeker ate a forkful of salad. "And what gives you the impression that we plan to just die on a full stomach?"

Talon smiled. "Bravado. I like bravado, Chercheur. I like you. But, your plans are irrelevant. Mine, on the other hand, are on a tight schedule. You caused a delay by rescuing the girl in Charleston, but now I have only hours to complete my contract and you are just simply in my way." The waitress arrived with two servings of beef bourguignon and set them before Seeker and Stephanie. As he finished eating his salad, Talon said, "I am a vegetarian." He dabbed his napkin to his lips, finished his glass of wine, and stood. "Please enjoy the rest of your meal, leisurely. While you will most assuredly die, there's no cause to hurry it." He bowed to the couple. "We shall not meet again." Talon turned and left the restaurant.

After Talon departed through the front entrance, Stephanie's hand, shaking slightly, reached forward slowly and lifted her champagne glass, taking a generous sip. "Damn it, Seeker, what is all this?" she demanded.

"About thirty dollars a sip," Seeker said with another mouthful of salad muffling his voice.

Stephanie punched his arm.

Several of Talon's friends reacted by reaching for their hidden weapons but stopped when they realized that they witnessed a lovers' tiff. Seeker noticed their reaction in his peripheral vision.

"Very interesting," Seeker said under his breath. "Keep eating but whisper."

Stephanie cut a slice of beef and took it with her teeth. "What's interesting?"

"Their reaction. Gives me an idea on how to get out of this Bat-cliffhanger trap."

"Bat-what?"

Seeker glared at her. "You gotta be kidding me. You never watched 'Batman'?"

"Sure, I've seen all the movies except the latest one."

"OK, sounds like I gotta plan a global flight with a long TV viewing schedule." He leaned over and kissed her long on the lips, then began kissing her neck, hiding his face from the other diners. "Hug me under my jacket, you'll feel five little pouches on my belt. Remove the middle pouch and keep it in the palm of your hand as you kiss me back... and then when I tell you, you start yelling at me about cheating on you and slap me as hard as you can, then you'll know when to throw that pouch on the floor."

As good as his kisses felt on her neck and collar bone, she forced herself to think. She watched through slitted eyes the restaurant staff walking to and fro, and The Talon's friends casting casual glances at them. Then she heard Seeker say into her ear, "Now."

She got to her feet, almost knocking Seeker out of his chair. "You damned sonuva bitch, who the hell is 'Leslie'? You screwin' someone else at the same time you're porking me?" She reared her arm back and swung her arm around hard, striking Seeker on his left cheek. The impact sent him backwards into the passing waitress, who in turn fell against the next table, knocking it over and sending meals flying into the air. The diners at that table reared back to avoid the food projectiles and in turn caused other patrons to fall over and send more food airborne.

On cue Stephanie hurled Seeker's pouch to the floor, and the smoke grenade exploded on contact. Within moments, the entire back area of the restaurant was a gray cloud. People began yelling and screaming. Inside the thick smoke Stephanie felt a hand grab hers and drag her out of the dining area and into the kitchen.

As Seeker led her out of the rear entrance, she saw that he was wearing his Task Force cocoon glasses, its embedded technology allowing him to see through the smoke as though it didn't exist. She also saw he had one of his Glocks drawn, and she used her free hand to pull the pink 9MM out of the holster at the small of her back.

He led her into a side alley and behind a couple of crates. They stayed perfectly quiet as several pursuing Talon associates ran past them, thinking the couple had run further ahead. Seeker reached into his inside jacket pocket and withdrew a telescoping dentist's mirror, extended it to its full three-foot length, and slowly held it out to the sidewalk. He rotated it back and forth gently, and, seeing that there was no one on the street, guided Stephanie to her feet.

She stood beside him, looking down the street both ways with him. "Now what?"

"Now," said Seeker, "we stop the Talon once and for all."

CHAPTER 8

SUMMER, 1991
NEW YORK CITY, NEW YORK

Sixteen-year-old Niklas Jungen peered out the portside window of the airplane and marveled at the stunning Statue of Liberty. He'd only seen a few pictures of it prior to the fall of the Berlin Wall last year before images of Western culture were allowed to flow freely once again into his part of the divided German city.

His grades in school were exemplary, and he advanced quickly and graduated high school a year before other students his age. As soon as the Cold War officially ended, his father applied for a scholarship on his son's behalf. Not only was the family collectively surprised when Niklas received the scholarship, but it was at a major United States university. An American commercial institute had hired his father, and a work Visa was rapidly approved so the family could move to the United States.

After the jetliner landed and all the passengers disembarked, the Jungen family stepped into the concourse of the John F. Kennedy International Airport. Hadrian

Jungen, tall and lanky with graying dark blond hair and blue-green eyes, took a deep breath and looked at all the people moving throughout the huge terminal. The family had spent the last several months learning English, and Hadrian's first words in America were, "Welcome to our new home, family!"

Elfriede was only five-feet tall and slightly overweight, but still attractive. At home, she usually wore her dark hair down, with a perfect flow of long black locks. In public however, she tied it up in a loose bun. Hadrian loved to run his fingers through her silky hair; it was the first thing that attracted him to her almost twenty years prior. With a much thicker accent she said, "Ah, the air smells perfect!" Her husband's new company had also secured a job for her in a German restaurant. For many years, she had been one of the best chefs in their native Berlin.

"No police," Niklas noted calmly. His clipped German accent was halfway between his parents in severity.

Hadrian pointed around the wide-open area. "Oh, there are police, but here they are simply security guards, not the kind who will be stopping us for no reason."

Elfriede noticed right away a gift shop. "Oh, we must get souvenirs of our arrival! Let's go find perfect memories!"

"Be quick then, El, we have to get the rest of our luggage," said Hadrian.

The family entered the gift shop, amazed by all the trinkets, books, magazines, and souvenirs. Elfriede spied the perfect thing right away. "Look! The American symbol is a bald eagle. Look, here are three little gold eagle talons on chains. Perfect!" Before her husband and son could reply, she took the three chains and charms to the register and made her first purchase with the American money they had acquired prior to leaving Berlin. After receiving her receipt and change, she handed one charm and chain each to Niklas and Hadrian. "We make these our good-luck charms as we start our new lives in this beautiful country!"

1992

Elfriede rapidly worked her way up to executive chef in Gehrhard's, a popular German restaurant in suburban New York. The owner also took an interest in Niklas and gave him a part-time job whenever he had breaks from college studies.

One weekend in the restaurant, Elfriede decided to prepare a new dessert she'd been working on. As she often did, she invited her family in to serve as her personal guinea pigs. Her latest creation was a twist on a classic rumtopf, using flavored rum to accent the natural vanilla taste. She had no problem serving her son alcohol-based desserts, thinking America was too prudish about age-limits on such things.

Holding her hands under her chin, she sat at a table with her husband and son, eagerly anticipating their approval. "So, what do you think?" Hadrian rolled his eyes and a happy grin crossed his face. The look alone was enough and no words needed. She was overjoyed at her new creation and would be proud to serve it to the customers.

"Mutter, this is incredible!" Niklas chimed in.

The restaurant owner, Gerhard Werner, a tall broad man with a love of food equaled only by his bulk, walked up to the family at their table. "Elfriede, I have a very special guest asking for dessert. What have you made this weekend, something unique, I hope?" He looked at the desserts she was testing on her family. "On the other hand, that looks perfect. Do you have more?"

"Of course, Gerhard, you know I'd never let you down with my new creations," Elfriede said proudly. She quickly returned to the kitchen and came out a minute later with a fresh dessert plate of her new rumtopf. Gerhard smiled and took the plate to the front table.

Niklas finished his serving and got up to go to the restroom. He kissed his mother on the cheek as he stepped away. "I love it when you serve dessert, Mutter," he said softly. "I could make a whole meal out of your treats."

She lovingly tapped his face with both hands. "My Niklas, such a gentle, sweet-talker."

On his way to the restroom, Niklas passed Amy, a light-redhead with an athletic build. She was a server at the restaurant and attended a table of patrons. He slowed his pace to give her time to finish and leave the table. "Hi, Amy," he finally said. He'd developed a huge crush on her over the last few months, even though she was three years older. The mutual attraction was no secret to anyone in the restaurant

"Hi, Nikky," she answered, smiling. Niklas loved the nickname she'd given him; he thought it was something special between them. "What did you think of your mom's new dessert?"

"That's the kind of food to take a girl out on a date," he said back.

Amy leaned against the wall and gave Niklas a hopeful look. "Nikky, are you asking me out?" she said, slightly teasing.

Not backing away from the question, Niklas took a step closer to her. "If I'm asking, will you say yes?"

Amy stepped over to the counter to pick up her next dinner order from the kitchen. "You won't know until you ask." Niklas smiled and blushed slightly as she walked away, taking that as an *almost yes*.

Niklas continued on to the restroom. When he was done, he opened the door, but stopped short when he heard loud, angry shouts coming from the dining area. The loud voices surprised him, the words creating a sudden wave of fear in his brain the likes he hadn't felt since Germany. He turned off the restroom light instantly so as not to be seen, opening the door just enough to peek out.

Gerhard was arguing with a man in a three-piece suit with slicked-back dark hair. The man was speaking in a language other than English or German; Niklas couldn't place it. He squinted hard to focus on the ruckus at the end of the restaurant. Gerhard was yelling back in the same strange language, and then stopped long enough to spit on the other man's shoes. The man looked down at his Mauri Patent Leathers in disbelief. Enraged, the man in the suit abruptly pulled a thirty-two-round .9mm gun from inside his suit coat and shot Gerhard in the center of his chest. Hadrian and Elfriede stood motionless nearby, clinging to each other. *The Suit* looked around the restaurant, seeing customers scrambling for cover, then back at the German couple, and grinned. Raising his gun, he shot Hadrian, and Elfriede in turn. All three lay lifeless in a bloody heap on the floor.

Niklas involuntarily fell to his knees inside the restroom and gasped in horror. Nausea stirred in his stomach. He grabbed a waste basket next to him just in time to catch the vomit. He began to sweat profusely and tears rolled down his cheeks.

What to do, oh what to do. Mutter, Vater, oh my God! He knew he couldn't scream out, and he couldn't risk getting shot as well if he bolted out of the restroom to call for help. He felt helpless, peering out of the restroom door again. Restaurant patrons were screaming and Niklas heard running feet, people trying to escape the sudden violence.

The Suit was hoping for a reason to shoot again. He saw them, several people sitting at a table within a few feet, all huddled together. He watched them. *Sniveling cowards*, he thought. The family that Amy had just served lunch were shot one by one, without mercy or conscience. Now on a frenzied rampage, the man walked into the kitchen, aimlessly shooting at all the employees that were preparing meals.

The Suit exited the kitchen, hesitated, and started to walk toward the men's room. Niklas had a better view of his parents' killer, but realized he was in imminent danger. He let the door close on its own, and in the dark he went into a stall, locked the door, and stood atop the toilet. His pulse quickened and could actually hear his heart pounding in his ears. *If the man comes and turns on the light, maybe he'll see no one in here and leave,* Niklas thought.

The Suit reached for the men's room door, then stopped and turned to the front of the restaurant, listening. Niklas heard the sirens as well, and heard *The Suit* turn and swiftly exit through the kitchen.

All was quiet now and Niklas stepped off the toilet. He placed his hands on the door, and his head hung low. He wanted to take a moment to calm, think clearly, figure out what to do next, and think about the killer, and the carnage he left in the restaurant, and his parents. The man was only a vision now, ingrained into his psyche. Sudden desires of justice and vengeance swept over him. He knew he was too inexperienced in dealing with this caliber of person who deserved the same treatment he just gave his parents and all the innocent people.

Is this an American person? Was this not the free land that all promised? How can he be free to kill my parents in cold blood? he thought to himself.

Tentatively, Niklas crept from the restroom. Staying hunched over, he ran to his parents' lifeless bodies. Heartbroken and crying, he fell to his knees between them. He held onto their hands, looking up to Heaven. "Why? Why did you let this happen?" Niklas was devastated. He cried great sobs, tears falling on his parents' faces. He held their hands tight, not wanting to let go. Police officers stormed into the restaurant; weapons drawn. *The Suit* was long gone...

September 11, 2001

Niklas never changed the name of the restaurant after he took it over six years prior. Gerhard's brother, Paul, kept the restaurant open after the unsolved mass murder in 1993, but was ready to retire. He'd interacted and watched Niklas grow into a fine man over the years, with an excellent head for business.

They both came in at eight a.m. to discuss transfer of the restaurant's ownership from Paul to Niklas. They sat together at the table nearest the locked front door. Paul brought the deed and tax paperwork with him for the transfer and would later file it at the county offices. He also wrote up a bill of sale agreement, selling the business to Niklas for one dollar, just giving the restaurant to Niklas as a gift. Paul had saved up enough money to retire and live his life out quietly.

"Gerhard would have been so proud," Paul said as he ran his wrinkled hand over his bald pate. He looked older than his 67 years, between the pressures of keeping the family business open and raising Gerhard's orphaned children, and then adding Niklas to the family. Paul's German accent, which had become a light accent in the many years in America, came out stronger as he spoke to Niklas. "He liked you, you know. Though when he got your momma hired, it was the answer to his prayers, and then he met your dad and you—he could see his retirement for the first time. He knew you were perfect to carry on his restaurant. It's a good thing he can't see your temper tantrums though; and the guns, and all the crazy security you installed. Yeah. I know. You're just reacting to the killing." Paul rested his arms on the table, looking down, remembering the past. "But ya know, Gerhard woulda slapped you upside the head if he knew how much you've changed. Quiet-like, sneaking around, guns all over the place. He'd still love you, like I love you, too, like my own son."

Niklas smiled and nodded. Despite the passage of time, and in sharp contrast to Paul, his German accent remained unchanged from the first day he stepped foot on American soil. "Mutter loved working here, too, Paul. And I appreciate your helping me with the apartment rent until I made enough to afford it on my own. Everything I have to remember about Mutter and Vater is in the apartment, everything left in the last place they touched anything. I hope they would be proud, too." Niklas leaned forward with his arms crossed, and his jacket panel opened slightly to reveal the Ruger G-3 .9mm in a holster under his left arm. "I know.

I've changed, Paul." Niklas lowered his gaze. "I'm afraid, you know, of what could happen again. And I won't let it happen to anyone here, *ever again!* That's why I do what I do."

Paul nodded at the pistol. "How good are you with that now?"

Niklas answered without looking down, "The shooting range awarded me a marksmanship medal a couple months ago. I am prepared, Paul. I'm hoping they come back some day. I hope he comes back, *The Suit.*"

Paul smiled in semi-approval. He knew the trauma that Niklas suffered over the years. "Fortunately, there has never been a second such event since that terrible day." He looked at his watch. "Ah, our first meeting will begin shortly."

Niklas raised his eyebrows. "Another meeting?" He looked at his watch. "At 8:30 in the morning? I thought it was just you and I meeting today."

"Business does not work on banker's hours, Niklas. This particular meeting has always been done in the mornings before you came in, but since you're the new boss you'll need to know what's expected of you." Paul patted Niklas' hand and gave him a small smile and nod.

There was a light knock on the side door to the restaurant, an exit that led to the alleyway. Paul stood and went to the door, unlocked the three deadbolts, and opened it. Niklas stood, agitated at the unexpected interruption. Four men in pricy suits and patent-leather shoes entered, all wearing sunglasses. Niklas narrowed his eyes, put his left hand on his hip, the right hand gripped the butt of his gun inside his jacket. He thought the intruders looked absurd in the glasses and suits and wondered why Paul was involved with them. The tallest and largest of the men sat wordlessly at their table. His thin gray hair was brushed back and held in place with hair gel, and the wrinkles on his face gave a tell-tale sign of his long life. Niklas was angered; his ears turned a light red color at the intrusion, his space, his restaurant. The large man stared at Niklas, then back over to Paul, who was relocking the door. Removing his glasses, he gently set them on the table and sat back, arms crossed.

"Who's the kid?" he asked.

"That's Niklas," said Paul. "He's taking over the restaurant, as of today, you know. He has to be here."

"Taking over?" said the man. He turned his gaze back to Niklas and looked him over from head to toe.

Niklas in turn looked at the face of the man who killed his parents, Gerhard, and Amy. *The Suit* had returned and had apparently been returning regularly since he killed his family and friends. "Niklas Jungen," he said, doing his best to remain unemotional.

"You may call me Mister Kralle," said the man, extending his hand in an insincere greeting. Niklas took it, plotting hurriedly. "So, you think you can run this place…and do business with me?"

"What is your business with us?" Niklas asked coldly.

Kralle looked at Paul. "He's direct. I like that." Turning back to Niklas, he replied, "Insurance…coverage. My company makes sure yours stays in business. Never know what could happen in a neighborhood like this, yes?"

Niklas narrowed his eyes again. "You have a business card?" He didn't really expect to receive one.

Kralle chuckled. "I like you! You make me laugh. Tell you what, I'll give you a break because you entertain me. No premium this month while you change hands and you take over this place. Give you a chance to get your bankroll started, y'know? Hey, Paul, it's 5 o'clock somewhere, get us a bottle to celebrate, eh?"

Apprehensive, Paul silently complied with the request, proceeding to the kitchen for a bottle of chilled champagne. Niklas cautiously settled back in his chair, his mind infuriated, sitting at the same table with his parents' murderer. He looked out the front window instead of at Kralle and focused his thoughts at the stunning World Trade Center twin towers, calculating his next move. He heard Kralle say, "So, Niklas, you have plans to make this place better?"

Niklas deliberately stared out the window as if ignoring the man. He was about to give a crass answer but saw something outside that caught his attention. He watched in horror as an airplane crashed into one of the World Trade Center skyscrapers. "Oh, Kot! Look! A plane hit a Tower!"

Kralle and his men all moved from their places to the front windows to peer across the city. Smoke was billowing from the impacted building. "Holy shit!" said one of Kralle's men.

"We got anyone down there?" Kralle asked. "Call 'em and tell 'em to get scarce. The cops and fire guys will be down there soon enough."

The visitors were glued to the spectacle happening across the city, their hands and faces practically glued to the large glass windows. Despite the dreadful incident outside, Niklas saw his opportunity. He quietly got out of his chair and stepped backward. Gently, Niklas reached for his .9mm under his jacket. As he began to draw it from the holster, one of Kralle's men looked away from the window and saw Niklas. The man immediately pushed Kralle down behind a table, drawing his own gun to shoot, but it was too late; calmly, Niklas fired a bullet into his forehead. He fired twice more, killing Kralle's other men within seconds. Paul heard the gunshots and ran from the kitchen. A great dread fell upon him, seeing that Niklas had done the shooting. At the kitchen door, he stopped, peering out, fearing what he was about to see.

Kralle rose up just enough from his cover to aim his own gun, but Niklas was faster. He fired a fourth time, sending a bullet through Kralle's wrist. The man's gun dropped to the floor, Kralle fell backward and howled in pain. "What's the matter with you, you son-of-a-bitch?" Kralle demanded.

"You killed my parents!" Niklas seethed inside but his hand was rock-steady. "I hoped I'd find you again. Hoped you'd walk through those doors again. This time, I'm ready." A flash outside caught his peripheral vision, and he glanced up just long enough to see a fireball erupt from the second Tower. "It looks like the police are going to be busy for a while." He stepped forward and picked up the fallen gun and stood ominously over his enemy. "Get up, Mr. Kralle."

"You don't tell me what to do you little punk!"

Niklas pointed his gun at Kralle's forehead. "You don't get up now, I put a bullet through your head and be done with you."

Kralle scowled, but managed to get to his feet, holding fast to his injured hand. Niklas handed Kralle his gun, barrel-first. "I'm going to give you what you didn't give my parents, a chance."

Kralle immediately understood. "Ridiculous. You shot my hand! I can't shoot—"

"You have another hand," said Niklas, "and to make it fair I will also use my other hand." He slowly slid the barrel of his .38 behind his belt buckle and tucked his right hand in the back of his pants. "Paul, I know you're over there. Why don't you count to three for us? Let's have a friendly little game."

Paul protested, "Niklas, no!"

"Paul, this is going to happen whether you count or not. I'm just making this fair for Mr. Kralle."

"Niklas, he's a big man in this city! You kill him and his boys will rain down on you—"

"They'll do no such thing," Niklas said calmly. "Okay, Mr. Kralle. One."

"You little shit," Kralle said in a growl. "You just signed your own death, you piss-ant."

"Two."

Paul could only watch as Niklas said, "Three." Just as Kralle raised and rotated the gun in his left hand, Niklas grabbed the gun from his belt, flipped it over for left-hand shooting, and fired one bullet, striking Kralle in the chest. Kralle fell back against the large front window, sliding down the glass to the floor, leaving a bloody streak on the window.

Niklas stepped forward and saw that Kralle was still breathing, but barely. Air mixed with blood gurgled audibly in the man's lungs. Niklas reached into his shirt pocket and pulled out a gold chain with a charm. "You see this, Mr. Kralle? My mutter was wearing this when you shot her, in cold blood. You take it with you now, as you die, so she can know you finally paid for your crime." He knelt and wedged the charm into Kralle's dying hand. "And, Paul, you can spread word that his company has been 'bought out', but the boss' name will stay the same. You see," Niklas told Kralle as he took his final ragged breaths, "I'm taking your name, you old piece of shit. From now on, *I* will be 'Mr. Kralle'."

"G-God-da-da—" were the only words Kralle managed to get out. He closed his eyes, blood dripped from the corner of his mouth, and he took his final breath.

Niklas stood and checked his clothing, not wanting any of Kralle's blood on him. "Have a good time in hell, old man." Satisfied, he reached up to his shirt collar and dug out his own matching chain and eagle's claw charm. He turned to Paul and said, "How could you? All these years, dealing with the man who killed my parents, your brother? You betrayed their memory!" Paul had come out of the kitchen during the gunfire but remained in the doorway. Niklas aimed his gun at Paul, ready to fire. Paul stood frozen in place from shock and fear. Slowly, Niklas lowered his gun. "No, there's been enough killing this morning. And frankly, Paul, I'm out of bullets, so fate was on your side. I've got more important matters now anyway."

Paul bolted from the kitchen, a worried scowl on his face. "What do you mean, you're taking his company? How? Everyone knows who Kralle is!"

"But no one knows me. I will become the new Kralle, Paul. This felt good. I feel like a new man, by taking out this bastard. I can do this. I can do it." He turned to Paul. "Tell everyone that the old Kralle is dead, but 'Die Neue Kralle' is alive and well." He reached down to the table, picked up Kralle's sunglasses, and put them on. He stepped up to a wall mirror next to the front door and looked at himself, pleased at what he saw. "Yes, 'The Old Talon' is dead, and 'The New Talon' is alive and well."

TODAY
BUENOS AIRES, ARGENTINA

Task Force Agent Seeker drove the black Task Force car into the cargo hold of his personal 747 airliner, *The Adventure*. Seeker and FBI Special Agent Stephanie Anderson exited the car, greeted by the flight engineer. "Good day, sir; Agent Anderson. Welcome back to *The Adventure*. I take it all went as planned?"

"Absolutely." Seeker stated as he closed the driver's door and opened the trunk.

"Very good, sir. I'll take a few minutes to chock the car, give it a quick inspection, and refuel it for you before we take off."

Stephanie looked at Seeker, "You got a freekin' gas station on this plane, too?"

Seeker smiled. "Yep. Right next door to the ice cream parlor."

"You know, Seeker," said Stephanie as the pair walked toward the circular stairs, "if you told me a week ago that I'd be flying in a plane that's a combination home, office, armory, and garage, I woulda called you crazy. I'm learning new things every minute I'm with you."

"And I hope to keep it that way, my beauty."

The flight engineer proceeded to set in place the automated tire-lock system, moved the galvanized steel chocks and running bars into place to keep the car from moving when the plane was in flight. A couple of Seeker's on-board staff hurried to the car's trunk to retrieve their luggage and take it to the 747's main bedroom one level up.

They sat at the oval conference table. Seeker placed his black duffel bag on the table as he sat. He looked down at his sports coat, lifted a lapel to his nose and sniffed. His brow scowled slightly. "I gotta talk to Mark about descenting those smoke bombs," he muttered under his breath.

"Who?" Stephanie asked.

Seeker closed his eyes and cursed himself. *Dammit, shouldn't have said that,* he thought. "No one important," he said aloud, "just a guy at Task Force who's really good with the tech."

Stephanie ran her fingers through her long sandy blonde hair and sighed. "That's twice we were in arm's reach of The Talon, and twice he's gotten away," she said, exasperated. "I'm gonna be the laughingstock of the department when I get back."

Seeker rested his head back on the top of his chair and let the tension flow out of his neck muscles. "Third time's the charm, my beauty," he said.

She looked at him. "'Third time'? How the hell do you know there's gonna be a third time?"

"He told us when his next appearance will be."

She gently put her hands on the tabletop. "He did no such thing, Seeker."

"He said, and I quote, 'I have only a few hours to complete my contract', unquote. So, whatever he's got going on will happen in the next few hours."

"Oh," she said, "I should've caught that."

"I'll let you take all the credit back at your office."

"You're such a gentleman," she replied, her voice just slightly teasing. "But, you're the big mystery type, so what's your next plan?"

Ms. Murphy entered the conference room from the stairway from the second level. "Here's everything happening in Buenos Aires in the next twelve hours, sir," she said, handing him several pieces of paper.

Stephanie's mouth opened in surprise. She quickly composed herself and said, "Are you some kinda mind reader, Ms. Murphy?"

Ms. Murphy cocked her head at Stephanie, smiled, and left the way she came in. Seeker did his best to not smile, but a grin crept across his face anyway.

"Oh, you think you're so damn funny, all your Task Force secrets and know-it-all staff." Stephanie sat back in her chair and huffed. She looked at him from the corner of her eye and smiled when she saw him smiling back.

"You're a very sexy pouter," he said. "But, fun will have to wait. I know where he'll be, and when he'll be there… we just have to figure out how to catch him in our trap."

9:00 a.m.

An American couple approached the entrance of the American Embassy in Buenos Aires and presented documentation to the security guard. The man was tall with light-brown hair and a matching mustache, his lady had short strawberry-blonde hair. Both wore tourist-style sunglasses and carried backpacks over both their backs. After the guard scanned over their identification he allowed them to pass and enter. The guard at the reception desk stopped them and asked to see their documentation as well, but this time instead of his identification papers, the disguised Seeker presented his Federal Task Force badge. "The ambassador is expecting us. We need to see him immediately."

They met the ambassador on the second floor, exchanged greetings, and he quickly escorted Seeker and

Anderson to a private changing room adjacent to his office. They got out of their civilian disguises; Seeker dressed his muscular frame into his Task Force uniform. The possible threat was great enough that it would be risky not to be prepared. As a standard, their uniforms were made of a high-tech black material, virtually bulletproof and form-fitted for each agent. The accouterments included everything else in black: boots, leather belt, holster, computerized cocoon glasses, and all the weapons and gadgets for any situation.

Anderson dressed into a pair of black slacks, black blouse and jacket, and black leather boots. She dressed more conservatively, yet she was also well armed. They returned to the ambassador's office as Seeker donned his computerized glasses.

Ambassador Jackson Crocker received the two agents in their new guise. "Damn, but if you two don't look like movie figures!"

Seeker shook his head. "First Steph, now you... where did this 'movie figure' tag come from?"

Anderson smiled. "Have you ever bothered looking in the mirror dressed up like that?"

"OK, fine, I'll tell the boss to design some new uniforms." Seeker scowled at Anderson. "And not one damn word about adding capes."

"Well, shit, that was my biggest fantasy."

Ambassador Crocker said, "I hate to interrupt this funny dialogue, but would you two mind explaining what's going on here? Aside from almost abusing my hospitality."

Seeker stepped toward the ambassador, sticking his thumbs under his gun belt. "The Talon."

Crocker's eyes widened. "Are you serious? The Talon is in Buenos Aires? What's he want here?"

Seeker removed his thumbs from his belt and crossed his arms. "Honestly, we're assuming a lot. We crossed paths with him last night, barely escaped alive. But he let it slip that he had a job to do in only a few hours. My staff correlated all the events happening in this city today and the only one they found was here; you receiving a group of transfer students from the States. We're not entirely sure of what he plans to do, but I'm pretty sure that it has something to do with your meeting with these kids this morning."

"So, what's your plan?" Crocker asked.

Once the embassy staff got over Seeker's unusual garb they worked with him and Anderson on the security controls for the arriving students. Seeker changed the patrol routines for every security staffer, altered directions employees took as they did their normal duties. No one was allowed to do anything habitual; even taking a trip to the bathroom involved walking away from the bathrooms before actually going to them.

Seeker stood in the main entrance with Anderson and Crocker. The ambassador, his gray suit perfectly pressed and his graying brown hair neatly brushed back, watched every employee pass them on their business. "This doesn't look right," he said with a smile. "All my employees seem to be out of place."

Seeker said, "The Talon is a great planner. He thinks ahead, like a chess master. He puts pieces in place before the game ever starts. I doubt he could anticipate that we'd not only move the starting pieces but change the game board."

Anderson watched the employees as they came and went, the security receptionist watched all the movement, the guards at the entrance watched the doors. "Partner, you get the same feeling?" she asked Seeker.

The Task Force agent took a deep breath and let it out angrily. He spoke through gritted teeth, "Yes, dammit. We've missed something. Whatever he's got in mind, Talon's plan is already underway."

The ambassador looked at both agents. "All this was for nothing?"

Seeker and Anderson exchanged knowing glances. Then Seeker leaned close to Crocker and whispered softly, "This is exactly what we counted on."

CHAPTER 8

ENDGAME

Nicarno Vega entered the embassy building the same way he did every morning: through the staff entrance at the rear. The thin, medium-weight chef placed his hat in his locker along with his light denim jacket. As always, he placed his athletic bag at the edge of his work area so he would have easy access to the special herbs he grew at home. He hated commercial herbs and spices, saying all the preservatives food manufacturers used made the herbs smell like sewage. He removed small jars of dill and cilantro to prepare the day's meals for the ambassador, his family, and the embassy staff.

Seeker walked through the library, then the conference rooms, finally stopping at the kitchen. His glasses contained a wireless camera which transmitted what he saw, and earlier synced to a private-channel television in the ambassador's office. "Do you see anything here that is remotely out of the ordinary?" Crocker asked quietly, but Seeker's ear comm picked it up cleanly.

Crocker watched the video feed as Seeker turned his head from side to side, viewing everything he saw. Crocker studied the screen closely. Finally, he said, "Aside from everyone taking different routes to wherever they're going, nothing unusual."

"Son of a bitch," said Seeker. He saw the security guards start allowing the morning group of students into the embassy for its tour. He hid away from the students, pulled his cell phone from his weapons belt, and punched a special number on the screen menu.

A deep male voice answered. "Go, Seeker."

"Spy, I need a suggestion." Seeker quickly explained everything he and Anderson and Crocker had done in preparation for The Talon's unknown plan. "In my gut, I know there's something still not right, but I just don't see it this time, boss."

Task Force Agent "Spy", leader of the Task Force field team, replied, "Seeker, remember, sometimes it's not what's in place as usual, but what's out of place in its place."

Bobby Morris was a 4.0 high school student and was excited for his opportunity to be an exchange student to Argentina. His excitement, however, was destroyed when he got the FaceTime message on his iPad from home, the video feed showing his parents held at gunpoint in their home in Kentucky. A man, who identified himself as "The Talon", visited Bobby in his hotel room. He threatened Bobby, telling him not to say a word, but do one "chore" for him, and his parents would live, and their captors would leave.

All Bobby had to do was exchange an item in the embassy with a matching one already there. Bobby knew he had no choice but to comply.

Anderson watched the students on the security cameras. They all wore backpacks which passed inspection, but she noticed one student was instead carrying an athletic bag. She touched the comm unit in her ear to connect to Seeker's comm. "Hey, hero, I see something."

Per Task Force protocol, Seeker did his best to remain hidden while in uniform. The covert nature of the Task Force Division demanded its invisibility to the world, and a couple dozen high school students seeing him was the last thing he wanted. However, when he spotted the one student with the different carry-all he decided to risk exposure…but to a point. In the privacy of a staffer's office, he borrowed a sports coat (just a little too large, but a minor detail) from a closet, pulled off his black leather elbow-high gloves, and tossed his weapons belt onto the office couch before stepping out into the hallway. The students passing him accepted him, in his black cocoons, as some kind of security agent.

He saw the student that Anderson saw. Seeker moved to intercept him and pull him from the group with no fanfare. "Open your bag," Seeker said softly.

Bobby opened his duffel bag and showed Seeker the contents: a couple of textbooks, including one about the history and culture of Buenos Aires, packs of crackers and candy bars, and a digital camera. Seeker removed the camera from the bag, tapped an interface control on his glasses, and confirmed that it was indeed nothing more than a plain old digital camera. He returned the bag to the student. "Proceed," he said, controlling his frustration at finding nothing. He tapped his ear comm as he returned to the staffer's office to retrieve his equipment. "Steph, the kid's bag was clear."

"Shit," he heard in his ear. "I was sure that was it."

Seeker removed the coat and pulled his gloves back on and reattached his belt around his waist. He reached for the office door, and casually noticed himself in the mirror on the back of the door. His eyes fell on the reflection of his belt buckle emblem, the circle-in-a-circle design, and thought of the diamond emblem his boss, The Spy, wore on his buckle's surface. He recalled Spy's advice earlier: "What's out of place, in its place."

"'Out of place, in its place'," Seeker repeated aloud. Throwing protocol to the wind, he stepped out of the office and now cared less if students saw him or not. He motioned one of the embassy security guards over with his hand. "Where are the kids going from here?" he asked the guard.

"First they're being escorted to have pictures with the Ambassador, then a presentation in the library, lunch in the cafeteria, then a conference call with the president in the main conference room."

"Which president?" Seeker asked.

"You're kidding," said the guard.

Seeker scowled, his anger evident. "Do I look like I'm kidding?"

The guard decided it was not the time to be humorous. "The American President, sir."

"Take me to the conference room."

The guard took Seeker to the conference room, and the Task Force agent quickly looked at every chair, table, corner, and piece of electronic equipment. "Nothing, dammit," he said.

Anderson said in his ear via his comm unit, "Video surveillance is clean across the board, Seeker."

"What we're looking for is in plain sight," said Seeker. "Keep scanning the feeds, especially anywhere the kids have been... or are going."

Seeker followed the students discreetly, watching them as they walked behind their tour guide, looking for any unusual movement by them or around them. When they got to the kitchen area the students were invited to enter and observe the preparation of foods, many unusual and unique to the embassy's menu. The kitchen's walking area was narrow, so the students were invited by their guide to leave their backpacks in the hall for a few minutes.

Chef Vega noticed the backpacks and the athletic bag being left in the hall by the students. He reached into his own bag for another container of home-grown spices.

One of the embassy staff guards approached and leaned against the counter by the spice bag. "Smells yummy, eh, kids?"

Anderson kept looking at every monitor in the security office, only taking a second to see the image before going to the next one.

She watched the children leave the kitchen, retrieve their backpacks, and the hall guard give the athletic bag to Bobby. As the students continued to the next part of the tour, she noticed—

"Seeker, get to the kitchen!" she yelled aloud as she bolted from the monitor room.

Seeker was in the kitchen moments later. He saw the black athletic bag in the hall where Bobby had left it. He was opening it as Anderson ran to him. "Textbooks, snacks," Seeker said. He looked at her. "You called me about a bag left behind, one that I already checked?"

"No," she said, "he was given his bag by a guard. A duplicate bag, I'd bet. No other kid was given his bag back."

Seeker looked around, remembering Spy's suggestion. He noticed that Chef Vega's bag was gone, as was Chef Vega. "Where did the chef go?" he asked the other cooks in the kitchen. The cooks all looked around the kitchen but couldn't answer him. Seeker told Anderson, "Go outside, see if you can find him, ask any of the security."

Anderson ran off to the entrance while Seeker went after the students. He caught up to them as they arrived at the library for their pictures with the ambassador. Bobby was first in line and placed his athletic bag on a chair as he approached the ambassador for his picture.

Seeker got to the door, attracting all the students' attention in his strange black uniform, cocoon glasses, and gun belt. He ignored their "wows" and "cools" as he swiftly surveyed the room and saw the bag in the chair. He moved to it without acknowledging the ambassador, his staff, or Bobby. Seeker cautiously opened the bag; as soon as he saw the blinking detonator lights he yelled, "Everybody, out!" He removed one of the pouches from his gun belt and threw it to the floor as he leapt onto the ambassador and student, pushing them down to the floor.

Anderson and the yard security guards all turned in disbelief at the explosion that blew out the wall where the library was located. Everyone drew their guns and ran to the now open hole in the side of the building. Some of the guards immediately began locking all the entrances to the grounds. "Seeker!" Anderson yelled. Her heart sank, knowing no one could possibly have survived the explosion. She approached the rubble and flames. "Dammit, Seeker, answer me!"

Security staff members were already battling the flames with fire extinguishers, and marine guards seemingly appeared out of nowhere to assist and move the students to another location in the building.

Anderson made her way through the debris and flames into what was left of the library. "Seeker!" she yelled again. She pulled a flashlight from her pocket as she searched through the smoke and dust, her gun pointed forward. She and the others immediately found themselves in front of some sort of wall that had not been there earlier. "What the hell is this?" she asked, touching the surface that felt like stone. The guards were just as confused as she.

"Ma'am, I truly don't know where *that* came from or what it is. It wasn't there a few minutes ago," one of the guards answered.

Shining the flashlight on its surface, they began to hear a faint cracking sound, and watched in amazement as the wall began to split in snake-like fissures from the top to the bottom. Backing away, they looked on as the strange rock-like object suddenly crumbled into thousands of pieces, falling to the ground. Within moments, there was nothing more than a spherical area of white dust, and in the middle were equally dusted Crocker, Bobby, and Seeker. Anderson stepped forward, boots crunching on the demolished wall. She crouched, staring at the three.

Seeker looked up at Anderson, his glasses covered in dust, but the special electronics inside his glasses allowed him to see perfectly. Anderson's mouth fell agape. "Well, hello, my beauty," he said. "I guess you're wondering about this."

She shook her head back and forth. "I'm not believing what I'm seeing. Don't tell me, it's a classified Task Force secret weapon," she said as she holstered her gun.

"OK, I won't. But that's the first time it was used in action; can't wait to tell the boss it worked perfectly." Seeker got up and helped Crocker and Bobby to their feet. "You two okay?"

"We're fine," said Crocker. "Thank you! It's obvious you saved us, but how in the world?"

"Sorry. Ah, classified," said Seeker with a sheepish grin. "C'mon, Steph, let's go."

"Go? Go where?"

"It is done," The Talon said into his cell phone as he sat at his table in the La Vache Française restaurant. "The ambassador is dead. The bomb went off one minute ago as planned."

"Are you certain?" asked the voice on the other end of the call.

"There can be no doubt. Everything was planned perfectly. My inside plants took months to secure the trust so that they would never be suspected. No one bothered to check the chef's bag anymore, and the hall guard worked his way up to a position of authority. No one could suspect them of being my employees, and while I hate the loss of the boy, some sacrifices must be made to accomplish the goal." His phone beeped and he looked at the display and smiled as he resumed his call. "Ah, I have received confirmation that my fee has been deposited. It was a pleasure doing business with you. Good-bye." He pressed the "end" button on the display screen and hit the number five button to start a new call. "You may release the parents, tell them their son did a fine job for me. Don't tell them he's dead, they'll find out soon enough." He ended the call and placed the phone in his inside jacket pocket. He picked up his glass of wine and took a sip.

A few minutes later a waitress came to his table. "Another bottle, monsieur?" she asked in a distinctive Southern accent. Talon looked up into the eyes of Stephanie Anderson. "Oh, don't bother moving. We brought along some friends of our own." She nodded her head to indicate the squad of marines at the entrance. "Any of your friends so much as hiccups; you'll all be dead in no time flat."

The Talon didn't react beyond his normal calm self. In his quiet German accent, he spoke up. "Agent Anderson. Please, sit, and join me in celebrating a contract completed. And where is your boyfriend?"

He felt a tap on his shoulder and turned his head to look into the barrel of a .45 automatic. "You may want that bottle; could be your last one for a long time," said Seeker.

Talon looked up at Seeker, his black uniform covered in fine white dust. "You look like you've been in an explosion, Monsieur Chercheur."

"Yeah, it was a bang-up event."

Talon looked back and forth between Seeker and Anderson. He narrowed his eyes when he looked at Seeker. "I suppose then that the ambassador is alive, as is my teenage pawn." He looked at Anderson and offered a small smile, then sighed. "Yes, my perfect plan did not include you, and when you found me here I did not modify my plan as it was already in motion. The odds were against you being able to stop me." He took a sip of wine. "I suppose I'm getting careless as I get older. Never failed a contract in all these years." He finished his wine and stood, placing his hands behind his back. As Seeker put handcuffs on his wrists, Talon asked, "Just how did you find me so quickly?"

"As my boss says," replied Seeker, "everybody tends to overthink things. You have a habit of dining here, so much so that you don't even think about it aside from planting your bodyguards here in advance. And frankly, all we did was call and ask if you were here or were coming here. You didn't even bother to tell the employees to say you weren't here if anyone asked."

The Talon simply nodded. "Yes. Yes, indeed. I did become complacent. Well, I suppose I shall have time to consider my mistakes for next time, yes, agent?"

"Lieutenant, take this piece of shit away," Seeker said to the nearest marine officer.

Another officer hung up from his cell phone and reported to Seeker, "Chef Vega was captured outside the city and is being brought back in for questioning."

"Excellent work," Seeker replied. As Talon and his men were led out of the restaurant, Seeker holstered his gun and turned to Anderson. "Now, where were we before we were interrupted?"

Anderson holstered her own weapon. "What?"

"We were in the middle of a nice dinner." Seeker sat and picked up the wine bottle.

Anderson sat beside him. "Are you crazy? You can't eat in public dressed like that! And you're covered in dirt and debris. Not exactly what a romantic dinner should look like, Seeker."

Seeker pulled off his black leather gloves and set them on the table. "So, how'd you like this little adventure?"

Anderson smiled and chuckled. "Y'know, I enjoyed it. I actually enjoyed it. Best vacation I've ever had. Certainly the most unusual, but being with you made it perfect. I'm ready for our next adventure together." She leaned over and kissed his dusty cheek before sitting down beside him.

"Good. Now, before another adventure decides to interrupt us…" He reached into the black pouch above his holster and brought out a little velvet box. He opened it and presented the diamond ring to her. "Would you be interested in becoming Mrs. Calvin Geffers, my beauty?"…

ABOUT THE AUTHORS

JACK GANNON

Jack Gannon began his literary career with high school best friend Cyndi Williams-Barnier after they were both retired from their respective careers, writing the stories they talked about way back in high school.

YBR Publishing was born when Jack wrote and published his first solo book, "I WALKED IN SANTA'S BOOTS", a coffee-table-sized autobiography about his quarter-century as Santa Claus for Beaufort, SC. "SANTA" was entered into the Beaufort County Library Historic District Collection as an important book reflecting the history of Beaufort, SC, as well as the Columbia State Library as an important book in South Carolina history.

His decades in print media gave him the experience to put together that first book in a unique and attractive scrap-book style, and now serves as the Production Manager for YBR Publishing. Jack works one-on-one with each author to create a distinctive visual signature in the book from cover to cover, a trademark style individual to each author with YBR Publishing. In addition, Jack is YBR Publishing's webmaster and finance manager.

Jack also serves at St. Peter's Catholic Church in Beaufort as the Proclaimer Ministry chair.

He is retired from The Beaufort Gazette & The Island Packet after 24 years in management plus another ten years prior as a motor route delivery carrier and intern reporter.

In January 2021, Jack was double honored by Marquis Who's Who with inclusion in the Marquis Who's Who Top Executives and the Albert Nelson Marquis Lifetime Achievement Award for his lifetime careers in print media and publishing.

Jack lives in Beaufort, SC, with his wife Mendy; Tasia, a 15-year-old Pomeranian; and Mister Grey, an 8-year-old Russian Blue who is "a lot of cat"!

CYNDI WILLIAMS-BARNIER

Cyndi Williams-Barnier, a Beaufort, South Carolina native, brings to YBR Publishing 25 years of county government service in Emergency Management, including writing and managing grants, writing training programs and detailed multi-agency operations manuals for disaster preparation and recovery. Her detailed programs are still used as guideposts for county, state and federal agencies including FEMA, Homeland Security and the National Guard at the Pentagon.

As co-founder of YBR Publishing and co-author of nine books, she brings a unique personal perspective and experience to maximize marketing opportunities for YBR and its authors. Her eye for detail and creative skill brings the emotional connection to every manuscript.

Cyndi was awarded a plaque and flag flown over Camp Phoenix, Afghanistan, from the Department of Defense; plus, she was awarded a retirement plaque from the Beaufort (SC) County Emergency Management Division for her 20 years of service.

Cyndi lives in Ridgeland, SC, is married to Bill and has one adorable cat, Scooter (who serves as her personal YBR critic)!

www.ingramcontent.com/pod-product-compliance
Lightning Source LLC
Chambersburg PA
CBHW071202300726
48975CB00004B/1259